DARK FATE: A CHRISTIAN TALE

DARK FATE: A Christian Tale
Pinnacle, CA
Midnight Shadow Pack

*I lost my entire family because of my father! THAT is the
painful revelation. I wish I weren't his seed...*

Everyone I cared about is gone.
I lost so much more than I gained...
This chaos would never have happened if I had a say in
it.

I'd probably still have my mother.
I would live a normal life being the Alpha heir and head
of the pack.
Most important, I'd probably still be a Legacy.

How did I lose my Legacy status? Well, that's where the
story lies.

I am Christian Grey, son of Tomas and Mila Grey,
Alpha and Luna of the Midnight Shadow Pack.

I should state that proudly, but I don't. How could I
appreciate the people who abandoned me? My
grandmother was my guardian angel, who made me feel
love.

She was the sweetest person ever to live. She made even
the dirtiest chores enjoyable when she filled her small
cottage with the soothing sounds of jazz music early

Sunday morning. She would sing along, pulling me to the middle of the room to dance. She was the best part of me, and there was never a day she didn't tell me how special I was.

When I turned 18, I discovered she meant that literally. That morning my grandmother sat me down for a talk. I assumed she would kick me out. I was an adult now—time for the bird to leave the nest.

She assured me I would always be welcomed here, no matter my path in life. "But your path has already been mapped out for you. Sweetheart, there's a lot I have to tell you today, and I want to start by saying that it was all done in your best interest." I saw a flicker of worry in her eyes, maybe even fear. I think she feared my reaction because she had been holding back information that sounded important. She looked so weary from carrying whatever burden this was.

"What is it, Nana?" She grazes my cheek with her small hand.

She tells me I am a Legacy, a powerful hybrid of werewolf and sorcerer.

Usually, one appears before the other, it's very rare they appear together, but that's not to say it doesn't happen. For me, my werewolf Kasilious, or Kas appeared right before I shifted. He came from the depths of my mind, surrounded by smoke. It was a pretty badass introduction and the first shift felt like I was coming into myself. Now I awaited a proper introduction that would come in due time. I would not seek it but let it happen organically.

She continues, telling me that although I was living and raised by her, my parents were very much alive.

After the initial shock, I couldn't wrap my head around it to make sense. "So, you're telling me my parents are alive and had me hidden away because I'm a hybrid freak? Is that why they abandoned me? That's it, isn't it? They are ashamed of me!" I rather she had not told me, and I lived my life in the dark. Why did it matter anyway?

She pats my hand as only grandmothers do. The gesture soothes me and allows me to focus on her words and not the disappointment I feel I am. "Quite the opposite, dear. They were protecting you. You have a rare gift, a blessing! And the enemy preys on children and spouses. Legacy elder law mandates that we hide special children like you to keep them protected. Now it is your time, dear. Time to secure your reign as the next great Alpha of the Midnight Shadow Pack."

She looked at me proudly, but I was overwhelmed with all this information. And now I was supposed to lead an entire pack of strangers?! If she weren't my grandmother, I'd think she was crazy!

"Listen to me, Christian Evan Grey; you will do amazing things. You are destined to be a great leader; do you hear me? Do your best and make your Nana proud, okay?" Her eyes fill with tears and I wipe a stray from her cheek. "I'll make you proud of me, Nana."

She smiles and pinches my cheek. "Good, now go pack your stuff. They are on their way to take you back to the packhouse. It shouldn't be too long; it's not far from here."

I don't know what enraged me more, whether they were alive or so close. I thought it was a big castle up there when I was younger. As I got older, I suppose I outgrew the fairytale and thought it was some correctional compound filled with murderers and psychopaths.

"Wait, today?! I don't want to leave you here by yourself. Are you coming with us?"

She shakes her head, "Oh no, dear, I'm fine right where I am. Besides, it won't be much longer that I'll be joining your grandfather in the sky."

I saw her gaze at their wedding portrait sitting on the mantle and smile. Meanwhile, hearing those words sucked all the air out of my lungs, shattering my heart. She always had that intuition. She knew when someone close had little time left. I wasn't ready to say goodbye, but I knew her heart was still with Papa, although it had been eight years since his death.

It used to be that a mate died shortly after their mate because of the strength of their bond. But that rarely happens now. Maybe the Moon Goddess saw how losing both decimated families. I know I was terrified to lose both and be alone, but she saw fit to let me keep my grandmother.

It's the least she could do after putting me in this situation.

Seeing the pain of knowing what she meant, she placed her tired shaky hand on my cheek, "Don't you cry for me. I've lived my life and raised you to be strong, powerful, and confident. Now, I'm ready to be with my Clive again. All I ask is for you to find what makes you happy, not what people tell you is your happiness. Don't let people force you to be something you are not, ever!" She seemed very adamant on the last part and I nodded in agreement. Little did I know how life-changing that statement would be.

She let me shed a few tears, then insisted I get ready because they would be here soon. I know this interaction will be awkward and downright intense with all my emotions. You know, rage, anger, frustration, and unfortunately, disgust. If they are expecting a sentimental reunion where I'm excited to see them like a lost puppy, they are in for a rude awakening.

About an hour later, I had packed my trunk when my grandmother called for me. "Coming, Nana!" I drag the massive cedar chest down and stop at the bottom of the stairs. Two enormous men in black suits head my way. I freeze as they stop in front of me, grab my trunk, and carry it out.

After a sigh of relief, I focus on the two people standing next to my grandma.

Wow.

The resemblance is uncanny. My father was a towering six foot six easy, with skin like bold, rich espresso and the same deep hazel eyes I see every day in my bathroom mirror. His expression is stoic, strong, and fierce, like a man with unlimited power.

Maybe he does have great power. How would I know? Not like he raised...you know what, moving on...

My eyes pan down to my petite mother, who has the smoothest skin, like fresh cream, long flowing jet-black hair she had pinned halfway up to frame her oval face and almond-shaped eyes. When our eyes meet, I am drawn to the deep emerald green hue before she cries. I felt my throat tighten, I wanted to be stubborn and show no emotion, but she was my mother. She holds her arms out, hesitates for a moment, then steps toward me. She squeezed me so tight, but I knew it was because she finally had her son in her arms. I bask in her honey vanilla perfume, light, and regal. It suited her perfectly.

"Christian, my baby, you've grown to be so handsome."
She clamps down hard again and I finally feel my
mother's warm, loving comfort. Then my father
surrounds us, loosely embracing us. But that was short-
lived as he pulled away. "That's enough, Mila. I don't
want a weak son. Never ever show weakness, son. Time
to go." His tone sounds harsh. My mom shifts
uncomfortably, she wants to continue loving on me, but
she cowers under my father's gaze. She places her hands
in front and bows to my grandmother before she turns to
leave.

I hug my grandmother and she kisses my forehead.
"Don't you worry about me, sweetheart. You do good
things for the pack. Even if I'm not in this world, I'm
always with you. Nana loves you so much." Her eyes
filled with tears, and I saw when she glanced behind me
at my father. She looked...scared?

My father scoffs, "You show too much emotion, mother.
Let the boy be. I'll have to undo all your years of
emotional garbage. Come on, Christian, no time like the
present." He sounded so cold-hearted towards his
mother, his own mother!

I dismiss his suggestion and I hug her once more, "I...I
love you, Nana." She nudges me towards the door. "Go
on."

My mom and I head out, leaving my father with my
grandmother. Why did I feel this twisted sense of dread?

After what seems like forever, he comes out, climbs in, and shuts the door signaling the driver to go. I look back, but she's not at the window like I thought she'd be to see me off. I promised myself I would call her once I got to my room.

She wouldn't answer my call; she never answered any of them.

My life changed completely by turning 18.

After being welcomed by the entire pack, I took about a week to acclimate to the robust schedule my father had set for me, including the hours-long training sessions.

I usually dodged numerous fireballs aimed at my head by my father, or his sorcerer, Umbri. He surprised me once by throwing one that split in two and headed towards me from both directions. I had to react quickly and found myself flat on the ground.

His laughter sounds so malignant. Was he intentionally trying to hurt me? I know he was my father, but he's been only cold and heartless; who's to say he wouldn't kill me? For him, I had to prove I wanted to live, I wanted to be Alpha to *his* pack, and it was exhausting because as much as I hated to admit it, I needed his acceptance, and I would drag myself through the fire to get it.

After about three months of grueling practice, I felt he was becoming proud of what I had learned. Our sessions became much shorter as he also taught me the history of our pack and our family's significance as Amber Legacies.

"There are three Legacy families, Amber, Violet, and Jade. We possess the dual power of our wolves and, most of the time, witches, or sorcerers. There may be combinations with fairies, vampires, or other creatures, but mostly, it remains within the two species. There has always been an unspoken competition between the families and the packs for power. Legacy folklore decrees the family who bore the first child would possess the power twice as strong as their parents and become the most powerful creature in the world. A family who had that power could rule the world, son. The possibilities would be infinite! And each generation is more powerful than the last."

"So, who holds that power now, is it us? I am 18 now. I don't feel any different than before." My father does that dark laugh again before he stands up from his desk and looks out the bay window. The sky was dark grey with cloud-to-cloud lightning.

"No, son, you were born a year and a half too late, proving to be a disappointment to me already." He didn't even hesitate to put me down and blame me. "We are not the most powerful...yet. They aren't even capitalizing on what they have! They want to remain peaceful…cowards, but I have a plan and that's where you come in."

Thunder shook the house after he spoke; it was as if he controlled the storm outside. "Me?"

"Yes, you are next in line if I can't dethrone them. It is your sworn duty to take on the task of crushing them and becoming the most feared pack! That's why we practice for hours on end. We craft our skill and hone our power; it's not handed to us. And that will make our victory even sweeter."

I craved his approval so much I obediently agreed while still digesting the plan. It was insane, but his passion made it sound like it was the right thing to do, for our Legacy family, for our pack.

Little did I know this was a form of brainwashing. He knew I wanted his acceptance and his love. He used it to manipulate me.

Time skip: Four years later

"I'm serious, Chris, I hate to sound like a broken record, but you need to find your mate."

I chuckle as I turn to Fitz, my Beta, as he follows me to my office. "Well, I don't see you actively looking for yours, so why are you pressuring me?"

"Hey, I'm not running an entire pack. I'm just assisting you. You need someone to balance you, or this job will run you to the ground. Besides, I'm tired of you bitching to me about everything." I turn to see him shrug his shoulders.

"Ha, well, it's too late for that. I enjoy having fun; besides, I don't want to force it. I think about this daily, and I am taking the necessary steps to get closer to finding her..."

Then my double doors swing open and I hear that annoying clicking her heels make on the wood floors, "Chrissy, if you name me your Luna, you wouldn't have to worry about searching for some girl whose skills will never outmatch mine. Don't I give you everything you need?"

No doubt she was eavesdropping.

I see Fitz roll his eyes as he exits quickly, not even hiding that he couldn't stand her. I turn my attention to her; she's licking her lips as she leans over my desk.

"Bambi, I told you repeatedly not to call me that. We've been over this; you are not my mate. We're just having fun until I find her, that's it."

She stands back up straight, then saunters around my desk, nudging my legs apart before dropping obediently to her knees. She knows a sign of submission is my weakness. She rubs across my bulge purposefully to make me lose focus so I wouldn't kick her out of my office. "Looks like he says differently. Let me take care of this for you, baby…"

I hear Kas growling his disdain for Bambi. He only wants our mate and knowing we are with someone other than her, he makes it very clear that he hates her. He tries to break the surface to scare her off, but I catch him in time. Besides, leading this pack had me stressed and pent up. Who am I to turn down a courtesy blow job?

I close my eyes and imagine it's my mate, except it was missing those tingles that make your senses come alive. I dream of what it would feel like and how her very touch would set off an explosive train to a mind-blowing climax.

I'm panting as Bambi smirks while wiping her lip and depositing it in her mouth. Not giving her a chance to get comfortable, I escort her to the door. Bambi palms me one last time and walks away when my team follows me back into my office. I exhale as I adjust myself to make sure everything is secure.

Fitz shakes his head and I'm in for yet another lecture. "She's such bad business, Chris. You know she's telling everyone she will be the pack Luna, right? And they will believe her if they keep seeing her sneaking out of your suite space. Plus, she isn't the quietest when you two are...together. You need to nip this in the bud now."

Kirin and Kellan, my Deltas, nod their heads in agreement, but I brush them off.
What I say goes and I can guarantee there is no amount of liquor, drugs, or magic to make that woman my Luna.

She's good at what she does that's it.

I walk behind my desk and sit down. The twins claim the leather couch by the fireplace while Fitz sits on the other side of my desk, tapping his fingers, "Fine, we'll drop it for now. Let's talk about the upcoming conference."

Ah yes, it was time for the Annual Alpha Northwest meetup, and this year it was being held at the legendary Cheshire pack house. The pack is now run by Kayden Miller, whose father died suddenly this year. Now he was thrown the reins and learning simultaneously, much like me.

His father, Mitchell Miller, was an amazing orator and peacekeeper. Gone were the days of packs attacking each other for bragging rights. Those primitive days are what my father was used to, which is why he was always trying to gain power over the Violets or the Cheshire's but, alas, never did. He never stopped trying, though:

"I am in the final steps of putting this plan into action. I must make one final visit, one final sacrifice, and it should be the last piece to the puzzle. I will set off Saturday morning to ensure this plan does not fail, no matter what."

Well, I have no intention of carrying out his destructive plan against the Legacies or any other packs. We live in a world of peace and I don't plan on doing anything to change it. I only attack those who attack me first and there have only been two breaches since my reign and relatively recent, too. I know who it is, I am withholding from ripping him apart and splattering his blood all over the land, but if another attempt is made, he will see the side he's been looking for.

I speak of the interminable "Alpha" Damien, who was no true Alpha. He didn't get the crown passed down to him. No, he pieced together his pack from a bunch of misfit rogues and idiots who gladly followed his command.

Why is he snooping around my land and in my archives?

He wants to hold something over me, or he wants to see if I have the power of the Legacy. I won't divulge my Legacy status to anyone; it is a heavily guarded secret, but rumors spread.

I think he believes if he outs me, he'll prove his allegiance to the real packs and get the same respect as the true Alphas or the more likely reason is to team up with me so we could be powerful allies. It's a power-hungry move and idiotic. I would never align myself with someone who wasn't even an Alpha. He would fail in whatever hair-brained scheme he came up with. Besides, he's an egomaniacal crackpot.

I bring myself back to the present conversation, "Yes, I look forward to the tedious meetings and droning on and on, then we sign the peace treaty and return home. When it's my turn, I suggest a teleconference and digital signatures. Thank goddess, it's only a weekend. Do we already have my room reserved in town?"

"Yes, I reserved three suites. One for you, one for me, and one for the twins." We reviewed the details to ensure it's easy in and out. I don't care to socialize more than I have to. I've been called anti-social, but I'm clearly not as I attend and converse with my fellow Alphas. However, I don't go looking for events to attend after the mandatory meetings. My leadership and I may hit the club, but most Alphas are family men, so my particular lifestyle is something they 'grew out of long ago.'

And that's fine; I enjoy hitting the strip clubs. I love to watch but never touch. We even have a pack-owned club downtown in our cozy seaport town of Pinnacle, California. It's also an excellent business investment.

Leather & Lace, where all your fantasies come true. I admit it is unconventional for us to own a strip club, but

I would not let our she-wolves strip at a local place with no protection, mainly because all dancers must be unmated.

Could you imagine if a mate discovered their other half was dancing nearly naked at a club for men to leer at them? They'd rip everyone wide open and torch the place. I don't know how my wolf or sorcerer would have reacted had they seen her there. Instantly, I know the answer as it shows a flash of fire burning the compound to the ground. That was an extreme warning, and I guess it wasn't from Kas. There is still uncertainty about the relationship between Tavarious, or Tavi, my sorcerer, and me. Tavarious means misfortune and I thought his presence was my misfortune. I always felt I don't have complete control of him, and I secretly fear he might take over, but he assures me that his only job is to right the wrong. I agree with extreme caution.

Anyway, after we nailed everything down, I spent dinner, into the late hours, in my office. I was creating a solid security plan, not only for this conference but for when I visited the other packs.

Even though I'll have Damien in my sight, there's a great possibility he'll attempt to breach my grounds while I'm away at this conference and his excuse will be, *'Well, how could I possibly have done that? I was here.'* I can hear his sniveling, conniving, condescending tone.

I don't know why we invite this imposter to our events or enable this charade. I know I will not invite him when it's my turn to host. He can have whatever kind of tantrum he wants.

It was almost 11 o'clock when I made my way to my room. My office and suite are on the four-level mansion's top floor. Only the soft glow of the wall sconces helps me navigate the corridor. Thank the Moon Goddess, I have a private jet, but I plan to be there early so I can wander around the town where my hotel is, Lovenshire.

My eyes sting from exhaustion causing me to yawn while opening my door, but it's cut short. Bambi grins as she caresses herself over my silk sheets. "Chrissy, baby, where were yooooou? I've been waiting for you all night."

I flinch at her pet name for me. I have to force myself, or Kas rather, not to bare our claws and rip her to shreds. He growls in my ear,

K: Don't, she not mate, she bad business. Certifiable!

C: Dude, I need to relieve some stress. This is a good outlet and she'll let us do anything.

K: This bad idea.

C: I have to satisfy my needs besides this is the last time, promise.

I don't know who I was trying to convince, him or myself. Kas blocks me, which is his way of staying out of it.

Maybe I won't even regret this. I turned my attention back to her as she was keeping herself busy. "I told you not to call me that and you must be punished for your disobedience." I arch my brow and she purrs at the excitement of what I might do to her. She sits up and lets the sheet slip to pool at her knees, revealing her tight naked frame in the moonlight. She may have a voice that makes you cringe, but that mouth does amazing tricks, and I was looking forward to every one of them tonight.

"Bad girls need to be punished."

"Mmm...so much. Why don't I show you how sorry I am." She replies as she pulls me close, her lips ghosting mine as she unzips my pants and I lose focus and probably a little bit of my dignity.

The following day, I woke up feeling instant regret and something heavy on my chest. It should be guilt, but I looked down to see Bambi's arm and leg across me, her hair splayed across my shoulder and over her face.

Way to go, Christian. Fucking hell...ugh, I know I shouldn't have. I thought I needed it, but did I need it that bad?

I groan because she definitely won't leave willingly. No, last night's romp gave her even more hope of being seated beside me and she's about to take it and run.

This is the sign. I look down at her and I'm disgusted with myself.

I shrug her off hard, and she flips to the other side while I put my hands behind my head.

"What the hell, Chrissy?!"

I won't fucking miss her calling me that.

"Get out! Stop coming by my office, stop coming by my room, and stop telling people you will be their Luna. I'd rather take a wolfsbane-laced bullet than let that happen. Be gone by the time I come back, or I might let Kas rip you apart." I slam the bathroom door to solidify my point.

"You'll be back!" Then I hear her ear-splitting shriek before my bedroom door slams and I groan my hatred out loud.

I wash the guilt away and stand in front of the mirror, contemplating my life, where it's been, and where it's going. I need my other half, my sanity, the one who will complete me to make me a better Alpha.

Two hours later, my leadership and I are on our way to the Cheshire Pack. "They better have at least a bar in this one-horse town." Kirin jokes. Kirin and Kellan are seated at the table across from Fitz and me, who are in the leather seats. We are waiting for clearance from the tower to take off.

Kellen passes over a beer to his brother and two in our direction. I scoff, "Isn't it a bit early to start drinking?" I raise my brow to the twins.

"Well, it's five o'clock somewhere. Cheers to good times after the boring work is done. Thank goddess, only Chris has to go!"

They all laugh at my expense. While they're wandering about town or on pack grounds during their free time, I'll be locked away discussing the same old topics.

Every region in the U.S. has a pack treaty for all-encompassing tribes to, at least, keep the peace by region. Our area, the Northwest, includes Washington, Idaho, Montana, Wyoming, Oregon, and California.

I tip my beer, "Cheers, gentleman, to peace remaining in the packs. Let nothing create a ripple amongst us." We clink the bottles and take a sip before Fitz looks at me. "So..."

I know that inquisitive tone. I see my whole team staring at me now, asking the question without words. "Yes, I am ramping up my efforts to find my Luna. This pack included although I'm not sure this is the right trip for it."

"Could you imagine if you found your mate in the one pack your father wanted to destroy?! The powerful and mighty Cheshires. Let's be serious, he wanted to be number one whether it was by pack or Legacy. And since the Violets weren't focused on this one-sided feud, he turned to the packs instead."

"My father was power-hungry and for what? Being the most powerful or whatever puts a target on your back and a greater chance for retaliation. Once the dust settled on his death, I was able to ramp those efforts down and stop completely. I'm sure he's not happy with my decision, but what can he do?"

We arrived at the Lovenshire Plaza Hotel, a decently sized six-floor hotel. Since we had suites, we were afforded the top floor with panoramic views of the snow-capped mountain range behind the town. I must admit it's a nice view and I bet the slopes are sick for skiing.

I check my watch and have an early lunch in my room before I grab the rental and head to…

Attention Alphas, this is Kayden, to get a good head start to finish quickly, please prepare to stay overnight at the pack house tonight. For tonight only, we can get most discussions out of the way by midday tomorrow if we power through. Every room is prepared and of the highest standard. Dinner will be provided.

Great… so much for enjoying my room. After that revelation, I call my leadership to my suite.

"Alpha Miller wants us to stay overnight at the pack house, so Kirin or Kellan, one of you could stay here but don't have some slut in my room. *Or I'll rip out your throat!*"

Whoa… that last part was not me. They all look at me as I shake my head and rub my throat. Weird...

"Sorry, I mean it though, no funny business. Alright?"

"Y-yeah." Kirin says, his voice shaky.

"I'm headed over there now; enjoy your time off, I'll keep you posted. Here's my key, don't have too much fun without me."

I pack a small bag for tonight and hop in the rental. The drive is around 30-40 minutes from the hotel, it's your typical peaceful windy forest road which gives me time to figure out that little outburst.

C: Kas, was that little outburst your doing?

K: Not Kas, sorcerer out of control...need to lay down rules.

T: I was having some fun. You know, testing my range. No harm, no foul.

C: I didn't give you control or permission. Let's remember, I am in charge until I give over the power to you. Do you understand? Both of you!

I didn't give them a chance to reply before I cut them off. Kas was right, though. This is the first uncontrolled outburst, but not the first incident. That happened after my father returned from a secret errand my uncle Gregory was against.

A few years back:

When the SUV came back, only my father stepped out. He turned in my direction and had a smirk that made my blood turn cold. I swear his eyes glowed red momentarily before he blinked and looked away.

"Christian, my office, now!" He barked. His voice didn't even sound the same. It was off, something was wrong. I followed but kept my distance.

He faces away from me, staring out the window. "I set very high expectations for you, Christian, and I expect for you to take over this pack and rule with an iron fist. Excuses are for the weak and sacrifice for the greater good. That's what I did; that's what your grandfather did and every Alpha that preceded us. You don't know it, but you now possess the tools it will take to succeed."

He's right, I had no clue what he was talking about, but I sat there. He turns and his eyes are glowing amber. Soon, the glow surrounds his body. He smiles as I watch my body also glow. Internally I hear Tavi chanting 'thy will be done'. What did that mean?

I shake my head to focus back on the windy road towards the pack grounds. It was moments like those that made me feel weak and powerless. And a new revelation that Tavi has been disappearing to who knows where. I didn't even know that was possible. What could he be doing?

I arrive at the Cheshire gate, they check my credentials, eventually clearing me to go in. The driveway winds up to this huge estate, the house is substantially larger than mine, but his pack is also much bigger. I find a spot near the garage next to the other rentals, grab my keys, and am met by Alpha Miller.

"Alpha Miller, a pleasure. Thank you for hosting the conference and having me here."

"Alpha Grey, it is a great honor to have you all here, well, and Damien…" I chuckle and shake my head while we walk towards the door. "I don't know why we entertain him."

"If we don't, we'll never hear the end of it and he's harmless with his 'pack'. He could be our weak point to other regions, and we can't have that, so…we entertain the crackpot. Come on, let's go inside and get you settled in your room." I follow him and this place is insane! I am impressed with the rich mahogany floors and subtle accents around the living room and kitchen. There were several oversized leather pieces to accommodate a large crowd for a movie night. We pass the humongous staircase that no doubt houses Kayd and the rest of his leadership.

He points down the hall we are approaching, "All the Alphas are on the 1st floor, and we added security to do rounds inside in addition to the external, so safety is not an issue. The first meeting will start at 5 p.m., followed by dinner, then an evening session that'll introduce new business, and you know how interesting that gets."

We both chuckled because the last time was a four-hour session, and nothing got resolved until the last day. I can only hope for level heads and cool tempers, especially my own. I'm known to be … blunt and I tell it like it is.

He leads me down the hall to the third door on the right. I toss my bag and follow him back out and into the conference room.

It's going to be a long useless night.

Later, around 8 p.m.:

Gavel bangs

"Gentlemen, please let's have order. I will not ask again!" Kayd growls at us, but specifically to Damien. Chaos has ensued.

"I demand to know his status! Having that much power is dangerous; he could turn on us! Admit your Legacy status!" He roars at me, and it becomes deathly silent among the rest.

It is definitely not quiet in my head; I keep them both away from the surface. Kas is in combative status, his fur standing up and he's revealing his canines, threatening to rip Damien in half. Tavi sat there watching the theatrics like fireworks. I didn't know if his calm demeanor was good or if he was planning a big reveal by turning Damien into a lightning rod. Again, making me not sure of my control of him.

I stare at Damien, who is standing, while I remain seated. "Who or what I am is none of your concern. I will not entertain your childish rant like everyone else. I suggest you tread very carefully, *Damien*." I accentuate his name and lack of title to nail it home. It further pisses him off, "Why won't you answer the question, it's a simple yes or no. You're deflecting! He IS a Legacy and he's dangerous to us, don't you see?! He's an embedded danger! If he targets us, we won't know what we're up against!"

That triggered me as I roared up from my seat, lunging at Damien, but a few Alphas caught on and keep me from sinking my teeth into him. My eyes glow golden, signaling Kas was at the surface.

"You are only here as a joke! You're not even a true Alpha and to question one is blatant disrespect! You try to tear this division down with your baseless claims. If you want to talk about rogue behavior, how about when you breached my compound twice! But you know it's pointless...don't you, Damien? Because the minions you send never come back, do they? And as long as you keep breaking into my territory, they never will, and what's your end goal? Because you will NEVER climb the rank to be respected, you want to cause chaos. Be warned for the last time and with witnesses, next time it happens, I will sign a war declaration in their blood! And send the perpetrators back in mangled pieces instead of tossing them to the ocean! NOW, are we done with this charade? I'd like to get a decent night's sleep."

Kayden stands, "Damien, you will answer to the multiple breaches of Alpha Christian's compound first thing tomorrow, but for right now, this session is over, and we will start at 7 a.m. sharp. Dismissed!"

Kayden storms out first, obviously upset at this spectacle the meeting had become. I smirked when he addressed him only as Damien, about damn time.

The hours-long discussions and drama hit me hard. I wouldn't have made the drive back into town if I wanted to and it was better to have a room here than wrap my rental around a tree.

I look closely at my room and realize how palatial it is. A four-poster king-sized bed in the center with floor-to-ceiling windows on each side; on the left was a fireplace and the entrance to the bathroom. I was too exhausted to walk in there to change. I peeled off my jacket, t-shirt, and jeans and plopped onto the bed, willing my mind to dream of my mate...or at least give me clues to where she was.

I'm surrounded by lightning, but this is no ordinary storm. The dark clouds roll over the mountains with fury, a purpose. They seek to destroy any and everything in their path, but somehow, I don't feel like I'm in danger. I feel like I'm the one causing what is going on.

But not me, exactly.

I watch myself walk the grounds of the Cheshire pack as if I am searching for something. I'm walking past a stage and a huge barn-like building and then I stop in front of this smaller shed-like building with sliding glass doors. I step forward on the mat and the doors open, signaling the lights to turn on. Where is security? It should have triggered them to check why someone was in here so late. However, no one comes.

I step toward a glass case and see a huge book opened to a random page on top of all the artifacts. It looks to be the history of the Cheshire pack, but in a language I don't understand. I still flip through the pages. Not sure why. Then I hear a bolt of lightning hit close to where I was, and I'm startled...

I am jolted to my senses; I don't move as I try to figure out my location because I am not lying down in bed.

I'm standing. Outside.

I look back to see the Cheshire packhouse and, to the left of where I am, a platform. No, the stage.

"Just like in my dream." I look beyond the stage to see the small building I walked into in my vision. I didn't bother going in, scared of why I was about to fulfill what happened in my trance like state. What was I looking for? I don't think I've ever had an episode of sleepwalking before, why now? Something is not sitting right. I could hear Kayd's security call out their quadrants for security checks. I run my fingers through my hair while walking back as casually as I could.

"Alpha Grey, are you alright?" I hear a guard near my part of the hallway. "I didn't even hear or see you leave your room, sir." He was suspicious as he raised his brow, looking for a response from me. This could look suspicious, very Damien-like if I say the wrong thing. The problem was I didn't have an answer.

"Must have been during one of your bathroom breaks. I'm fine, trying to wear out this insomnia spell I sometimes get, especially when I don't sleep in my own bed."

He seemed to accept my story as I bid him farewell and close my door. I notice my patio door cracked open. I must have walked out and closed it enough so I could get back in from doing whatever I had planned. That was the critical question, what was I looking for? I close and lock it, hoping there are no more episodes while on pack grounds.

Day two wasn't as explosive as the previous day. The big news was Damien left before 7 a.m. to avoid answering for his crimes. Coward wouldn't face his punishment outright, but that's fine. If he attempts it again, I'll have every right to burn his pack to the ground and I don't mean his property, I mean each and every misfit. And I will.

Tavi: I found a punishment spell that renders them paralyzed but conscious. You can do anything you want and all they can do is watch. I can't practice on the dumb wolf, so why not an enemy, just say the word.

C: Then that'll give him all the evidence he needs. Think before reacting, that's why I'm in charge. Are we clear?

Tavi mutters something I can't make out.

T: Fine. Umbri was right...so weak...

C: What?

He disappears into the deep or wherever he goes, which is still a mystery that needs solving.

We had a productive meeting that turned into a working lunch to power through, it's not that we didn't like each other; we were just powerful men with very busy schedules. We discussed the major influential topics of the treaty, signed it, and last, chose where the next conference location would be. The Cold Mine Pack had that honor, their compound located north of Denver, Colorado. It felt good we could get it all sorted out within a day and a half and I know it's because we're not babysitting or distracted by nonsense.

I'm relieved to get back to my boys and my room. I open the door to an ear-piercing shriek and a naked blonde obviously straddling someone.

In. My. Bed.

"Oh, come on! I said no screwing around in my room Kellan!" It took some time for me to tell them apart, but the main tell wasn't in the face. Oh no, they were a spitting image, but Kellan had a giant tribal tattoo on his right arm.

Kellan's friend of the night covers herself, but I already saw her botched boob job, pretty sure her nips were lopsided.

I growled and she seemed to grab whatever she wasn't trying to put on as she hightailed it out of my suite. Kellan finds it amusing as he maneuvers his boxers under the covers then slides out and stretches while heading to the kitchen portion of the suite. "How'd the overnighter go?" He poured us a glass of orange juice and I sat at the island after linking the others to join us. I didn't bother wasting my breath about the girl, we were leaving today anyway.

He pours a tiny bottle of vodka into each glass. "Went better than expected. You can tell the flight crew we leave at 6 p.m. today. Don't need to ask you how your night went. At least my bed was used, I guess." I cut my eyes and he shrugs, "After that little outburst you had, Kirin was not touching your room, so I volunteered. I met her down at the hotel bar, I told her I was here for the conference, and she assumed I was an Alpha. To prove it I told her I had a suite on the top floor."

"I think it's safe to say she no longer thinks that. Besides she had lopsided nipples, that's very distracting…" Kirin and Fitz burst out laughing.

Kellan shrugs, "She was a screamer though, scratched me up good before I healed."

I held my hand up, I had heard enough.

"So, what was so different this time that you guys finished so quickly?"

I broke down what happened with Damien and his outburst, I forego talking about my sleepwalking episode and ending up in their archives. Basically, doing the same thing that Damien did but involuntarily.

Was I a hypocrite?

The difference is I have no idea what I was doing in there and the purpose.

We head out to the car and I catch a passing smell that reminds me of the ocean and... cinnamon? Kas' perks up a bit before I shut the door and we're on our way home.

No time for distractions. I had an unnerving feeling in the pit of my stomach.

A few hours later:

I'm glad to crash on my bed and unsoiled sheets. I shudder remembering that nightmare boob job. I wonder if she knew. I mean it was obvious.

This trip only confirmed how wild and carefree the lives of my leadership were. Consisting of four strong, healthy, single males.

It is not common to have an unmated Alpha. But I wasn't the only one, Kayden was also on the search for his other half, but he was taking it more seriously than I had. Some would think he was borderline obsessive. I'm not here to judge.

I rip off everything except my black jeans, unbutton them and fall asleep hard.

I don't know how long I was asleep, but a weird repetitive sound woke me out of my slumber and then an overwhelming tingling sensation. I opened my eyes as my orgasm rocked me from Bambi' surprise blow job.

"Ohhh fuckkkk..." I'm satisfied and irate that she snuck into my room after I explicitly told her we were done.

She giggles as she licks her lips, "See, Chrissy, you could have it anytime you want," She rolls over from between my legs to lay on her back, arching it upward, "make me your Luna. It's that simple." She pulls off her shirt, but I yank her out of my bed and onto her feet. I'm more than irritated at her disobedience. "Stop. I told you this is over, Bambi. No more casual sex, no more late-night visits, no more spreading these rumors about you being the pack's Luna. It's never going to happen! Let's be real, you were easy and good at what you do, that's it. Now continue that with the rest of the pack like you have been."

She gasped and her face flushed. I couldn't tell if she was embarrassed or irate, but I wave my hand, dismissing her fake shock. "Don't act surprised. You can't keep your legs shut or your big mouth. You'd tell anyone for attention, just like you fuck anyone for it. Face it, you're the pack whore."

I linked my security; she would not leave quietly.

"You arrogant son of a bitch!" Her eyes go black, but she doesn't shift, "don't act all high and mighty when you were screwing me...and you were usually last, too, since you want to insult people. Sloppy seconds, sometimes even thirds. You think your mate would approve of her Alpha bedding down, what'd you call me? The pack whore? Well, that title goes BOTH ways! Do you think that'd make her proud to be your wife? I can't wait to relay that little tidbit of information the moment she steps foot on pack grounds." She smiles a mile wide knowing she could ruin me with that and she calmly walks out of my door.

K: I say we rip her apart! Nobody miss slut.

C: We can't do that without reason, I'm not a monster, Kas.

K: If she ruin thing with mate...

C: She won't. And if she tries then we rip her apart. On to more important matters.

K: Like why human sleepwalk to book room? Sorcerer talks to entity Kas can't see, think he whispering but I have great hearing. He disappears with voice again. He up to trouble.

C: How long has he been talking to this entity?

K: Couple weeks. Started on anniversary of parents'
death.

What? Weird.

I am grateful for the time I got with my parents...well,
my mom at least. My father was down my throat from
the moment he laid eyes on me. I always assumed he
was ashamed of my progress and jealous of my
relationship with Uncle Gregory. I remember one of the
last things he said while he stormed into my father's
office:

"You're sacrificing too much of yourself, Tomas! You
can't do this! You have a wife and a son to think
about..."
Then the solid wood doors closed and he blocked me
from his link, so I had no clue what my uncle was
referring to, but it made me uneasy.

Whatever returned from the trip they were arguing about
was not my father. It was darker and even more adamant
about the destruction of the Cheshires or the Legacies. I
needed to figure out what happened and that started with
locating my uncle because he didn't return with my
father. I was certain he was keeping him away but now
that he was dead, he couldn't get in my way. I'll find
him.

Meanwhile, I need to find my beloved and so my search continues…

One week later, I am 0-5, and I have visited almost every pack and came up with nothing. The most memorable was my time at the Polyamory Pack…THAT was interesting. One moment I'm at home and the next day I'm in this free love, 'make peace, not war', hell here. This whole place smells like a marijuana farm.

There's a good chance I might be high.

"Celestial greetings to you and yours, Alpha Grey and welcome to the Polyamory Pack. Where it's all about loving each other and anything goes. If you wish to 'explore' with any of our members, please don't hesitate. Everyone shares with everyone..."

I shudder and pray that she is not here in this goddess-forsaken love fest. I'm not willing to share her with anyone. I'm not saying she should be a virgin, that's hypocritical when I've been having my own fun, but this free love crap is just gross. There's got to be stronger drugs than marijuana involved; no way anyone is in their right mind. This whole pack must be high on shrooms or LSD. I link my guys and tell them not to eat or drink anything here. I hear a few chuckles, but they agree.

Alpha Moonbeam...yes, I swear that's what he calls himself. He fits the description, too, with unkempt long hippie hair and a scruffy beard. I can only imagine what his wolf looks like. Probably dingy, dirty, and high as a kite. The name's probably Sparkles or some shit.

I hold in a laugh while trying to maintain my serious face, "Alpha, where are your unmated wolves?"

He spins on his Birkenstocks and grins, "Technically, we are *all* unmated." I think he saw my stoic expression and cleared his throat. "Sorry Alpha, follow me to our whimsical garden of bliss, the entire pack awaits your presence."

Sure enough, as we round the corner, there's a big open area with flower trellises and fairy lights everywhere. He twirls, humming as we head towards the crowd of 75 people, with most being she-wolves. They were scantily clad, dressed in only sheer all-white peasant dresses or skirts and a bra. They all had that same euphoric expression of total bliss.

One of the she-wolves bows and dips her body to welcome us, holding a large round tray of brownies. "Greetings Alpha, I offer you and your party some of our amazing 7th Heaven brownies. They're simply euphoric. Please, indulge in one or two and enjoy all the free love you can handle." I won't lie and say I did not stare at her double D's loosely wrapped in that sheer top; she's not wearing a bra. She pranced around each of us, offering the sugary and possibly spiked dessert.

There is no way I am eating that. I have Kirin take one to have it analyzed to make sure they are here of their own free will. I'm feeling cult vibes from this place.

"No, thank you." I finally reply as I stand in front of the group. I look each woman in the eye to see if I feel that spark or if Kas acts up, but he is radio silent, confirming that she is not here. That doesn't stop the women from trying to lure me into having my way with them.

"I'm sorry, Alpha Moonbeam, but I do not sense my mate here. We will be going now." I turn and head back to our convoy of SUVs. Alpha follows me and stands in front to stop me. "Are you sure you don't want to participate in our free love session? It starts in 7 minutes, you're all welcome to join." His tone is soft as he whisper-sings his words, elongating each one.

I already know by their expression that Kirin and Kellan are game. I see Fitz weighing the option, but I speak up, "I came for one purpose only. My mate is not here, I must continue my search. Good day, Alpha." I bow to him and he bows "Then I wish you blessings on your grande celestial journey to find your mate. If you change your mind, you can always indulge here... in your wildest fantasies."

This dude is creeping me out. I walk around him and once we are all inside, I exhale loudly. I look at Fitz, "Dude, what the hell was that?!" He shrugs as he shakes his head, chuckling at the mere experience.

As we pull away, we see Alpha Moonbeam in the crowd and the members shedding their clothes. I quickly turned away, but the twins continued to stare until they could see no more.

"Dude, you could have waited in the car!" Kirin looks hurt to be taken away from all the fun.

"Yeah, nothing like a drugged-up wolf orgy to top off your day. Come on, we are on a mission, stay focused on the goal."

"That is YOUR goal, nothing wrong with us having a few activities while we help you." Kellan backs up his brother.

"Listen, I know you were all for the fun and easy sex, but didn't everything feel...off? Like they weren't in their right mind? That's why I told you to nab that brownie, we're getting it analyzed. If this isn't the love fest it portrays to be then we'll gather the other packs to overthrow him and rescue the members. And if there is nothing in it then they're all bat shit crazy and that'll be that."

To relieve some frustration, after coming up empty yet again, and to not raise any red flags with Tavi, I insist on some sorcerer training, hopefully not giving him more power than he might already have. We spent some time outside casting spells. He knew some powerful stuff and the spells were particular. He was learning without my knowledge and I'm sure it's from this mystery entity.

Afterward, I shift into my wolf to allow Kas some free time and fresh air. Kas' was special in his own way with his iridescent black coat. It looked like the colors of the rainbow were trapped underneath the blackest black and that made me unique. Also, Kas was a wolf on steroids, he was massive. I enjoyed it when people saw me shift for the first time expecting the normal size and color wolf and gasp when they saw a massive black wolf with golden eyes.

Kas is full speed as we pass the main tree line and into the open field. He gallops, yips, and frolics, I don't judge what he does if he gets the exercise we need to be in tiptop shape. He finds his way to a small man-made pond on our property. He laps the water, replenishing our body.

K: When do we go back to Phoenix pack?

Phoenix was the name of Miller's wolf, he and Kas had a decent time while we were there.

C: We'll be there tomorrow.

K: Kas know she there. I smell her, you didn't let me speak.

C: Sure.

I didn't want to sound unsure or like I didn't want to find her but after this week I was feeling sorry for myself. Yes, the big bad Alpha doubted himself. Don't be fooled though, I can still rip my enemies' insides out and bathe in their blood.

Before the sun rose, I was up and headed to my jet. I greeted my driver, who took my weekender bag and placed it in the trunk. I get in and let my head fall back, letting out a huge sigh.

"Another big trip, sir?"

"Yeah, searching for my mate. I know it's no secret what I've been doing, and everybody talks, but we'll be so much stronger with her beside me."

He turns on some soothing music, "Aye, I wish you the best in your search." I close my eyes for the remainder of the ride to the airstrip.

Who knows how long later, but the sound of the door awakens me, "Alpha, we're here and the jet is ready for immediate departure. I already gave your bag to the steward. Have a safe flight, sir."

I get out and tip him, stretching my still sore muscles before approaching the airstairs. I text Alpha Miller letting him know I'd be landing in roughly two hours and expect me within the hour after that with his unmated ready for my inspection.

I should have done this when I was there for the Alpha meeting, but I didn't want them all in my business especially Damien. Once I had gotten home Kas told me he smelled her there and was trying to tell me. I felt guilty that I shut it down and headed home. That's why we're going back, I have to be sure.

Miller replies almost immediately, making me wonder what he's doing up at 7 a.m.

Two hours and a bit of turbulence later, I land at the Lovenshire municipal airport and there's a car waiting to take me straight to pack grounds.

Miller meets me outside and links his unmated to meet on the training field in five minutes.

As we walk over, he breaks the silence. "How has the search been for you? I, like you, am obsessed with finding my Luna and it has been a struggle for me, personally, especially with my father's death blindsiding me. Phoenix swears she's nearby, possibly in town which makes me think she might be human."

Obsessed?! I wouldn't call it an obsession, maybe that I'm determined. I silence my snide remark and go unanswered, only shrugging my shoulders.

We approach the platform to stand in front of 230 females. I walk the stage while scanning the crowd.

Kas sniffs the air and stirs.

K: She was here! I sense her but it's weak, she's not here now but she was! She was, she was, she was!

C: Are you sure, Kas? We have no room for mistakes.

He deadpans me. *O...kay...*

I turned to Kayden; frustrated in his lack to gather all the potentials as I had requested. "Alpha, is this the entire group?"

"No Alpha, I have a few who are unavailable for this impromptu meeting, a few of the ladies work in town at the hospital, the diner, and could not get suitable replacements in enough time, most of them stopped by earlier to see if maybe you had arrived early, but they had to report to work. Do you smell her here?"

"Not currently, but she was here. I am now certain that my mate is indeed in your pack. Is there somewhere we can discuss an idea I have? I'd love to go into town to look for her but with this discovery, I have a lot of steps to take back home."

I also wanted to get away from the building that housed their history. I felt a slight pull to explore but I knew that wouldn't be a good idea.

"Sure, we'll go to my office. Pack dismissed!"

We headed up to the top floor where his suite lay, much like mine. His office is on the left-hand side while mine is on the right. He opens his door and motions for me to sit on the sofa in the seating area by the fireplace. His office is about the same size as mine. He has a shelf of books behind his desk and a big window behind his chair.

My eyes are drawn to a magnificent painting on the wall. It was breathtaking as I gazed at a portrait of a girl pulling someone with her. Her facial features are hidden by her natural curls. As I stare at it, I wonder who she is? I notice his signature at the bottom of the portrait.

"Any particular reason you don't paint her face?" It was an interesting angle.

"She is my perfect girl. When I dream of her, she's always pulling me to the most beautiful places. I always wake up before I see her face. I know it sounds crazy, but I know it's her. She's, my Luna."

To be honest that would be quite the tale to tell. "It's a potential love story for the ages, Kayd. Now down to business...I want to return to narrow my search but, in the meantime, I would like to purchase a property here to solidify the bond between our packs and to use as I continue my search and after I would like it as a vacation home, does that seem plausible?"

He sits in the chair across from me, "Listen, the fact that you sensed her is leaps and bounds ahead of where you were. I accept you purchasing a place here, we have some new properties on the edge of town you can look at today or on your next visit. I also have a brochure, for now."

He hands me the paper and I peruse the specs of the homes. We spend the next hour discussing what I want down to the color of the exterior. I didn't need to see it; I knew it'd be done right. I transferred payment in full and my plan was underway.

I made it back to my hotel after lunch. I was excited to prepare for the arrival of my mate. Kas is anxious in my head, giddy with excitement at being so close to her. Constantly sniffing the air to get the slightest whiff of her. I assure him it won't be too much longer.

The first major tasking that comes to mind is to remodel my bachelor style room into a decent suite with a seating area and upgraded decor. Choosing fewer posters and biker memorabilia for classy/sophisticated items you see in William Sonoma ads. My interior designer will love it, she's been trying to get me out of bachelor decor for the past two years.

I always knew the design would change but in my moment of being wild and carefree it didn't matter what my room looked like, they come in, I give them an amazing time, and they leave.

Except for Bambi.

Another reason to trash everything in that space, the memories of her. If my Luna knew she was anywhere near the sheets someone else laid in, she'd castrate me where I stood. Better to start on a clean slate. I couldn't wait to get home to get the ball rolling.

The next morning, my phone buzzes annoyingly on my desk. I huff before answering. "Good morning Alpha Miller, to what do I owe this early morning phone call?"

It's almost 8 a.m., he must be an early bird, I'm only up because today is combat day for me and all my warriors, security, and ops teams. I was signing a few documents before going down to the practice field.

Most packs practice as one cohesive unit, but I find it to be counterproductive. The parents are watching the kids, telling them to stop misbehaving and focus. The teenagers are bored and half-assing their training because they don't understand how critical it is and only want to hang out with their friends or be on their phones.

It's frustrating as hell.

Now I separate by age groups and I keep my muscle with me so at least we are in tip-top shape.

Focusing back on my phone call he continues, "Alpha Grey, I called to let you know that your home will be ready by your next visit. The realtor will contact you to do a video tour to see if everything is to your liking. Also, when do you think you'll return? I'd like to help in any way I can."

" Next week, but it is quite alright Alpha Miller, I can make my way around your quaint town with my leadership. If I need anything I'll be sure to contact you, but I plan on being self-sufficient."

"Well, I wish you the best of luck in your endeavor. I'm excited to find out who it is."

"As am I. Have a good rest of the day."

I can't wait to get back so I can wander the town.

The week passed so painfully slow because of my eagerness to get back. Once again, we're on the jet headed back to Lovenshire. Kayden texted that if I needed anything to let him know. I thanked him for the offer.

We took the 20-minute drive to my new place. I noticed they had the windows open to aerate the inside from the new paint smell. It was a nice townhome and big enough for all of us. The guy's rooms were on the right side upstairs and I had a deluxe suite on the left with double French doors. I had connected with a local decorator and from the looks of it, she nailed the simple style I was looking for. I wanted it to look like a modern home for a couple starting out. I had the means to furnish it with one-of-a-kind pieces of art and the finest things but that's not the message I want to relay. Also, I want her to make this place our second home.

"Hey Chris, what's next?" I hear someone call out from the other side of the hall while I'm daydreaming. I felt I should go where I am comfortable in any town. "Let's find a club."

Within five minutes online, they located a bar, the only bar, Jack's. Looks like some country-western themed setup. Not my style but I couldn't miss our paths crossing. She could be in her tight daisy dukes and midriff baring plaid top dancing and having a good time when I stroll in and sweep her off her feet.

The outside of the bar is exactly how I imagined it, big wooden sign on a big wooden structure where the wood was worn and weathered giving wild wild west vibes.

There was even a hitching post out front. Do people ride horses to the bar? I chuckle as we stroll through the saloon doors and the entire place stopped.

I see them whispering and a few willing to shoot their shot at the new meat. They may not know me exactly, but they know I'm not some average Joe.

I move to the bar and order a bottle of Jack, a bucket of beers, and find a table big enough for us to fit. I miss having the Alpha advantage at the club like I do at home, luckily there are a few tables available.

The dance floor is packed for such a small town. The scent of sweat, lust, and alcohol hit me hard being so close to the dance floor.

There are some beautiful options, but my senses aren't flaring and Kas is quietly observing. She's not here so I'll enjoy the freedom of the night, maybe she'll walk in later, but for now, I need a stiff drink.

Kirin and Kellan are quickly pulled from their seats by some eager ladies wanting to try out the new options. Not too long after, Fitz is grabbed, too.

I think my aura screams Alpha or do not approach. I try to seem lax by looking around and bobbing my head to the music. It isn't all country music but a mixture of genres, thank goddess, or I'd probably put a bullet in my head.

"I've never seen you here before, new to town?" I met eyes with a blonde woman who got Kas agitated.

K: She reek of hooker. Think she town whore, she smells easy.

The nameless blonde in what was supposed to be a dress, but resembled a shirt, seemed to set her sights on me as a conquest or bragging rights. She leaned forward to showcase her pushed up boobs and licked her lips. And honestly...nothing about her was appealing.

"What's your name, handsome?"

I had time and humored her.

"Christian, and you?"

"I'm Bridget, so...what brings you here to this crap little town? This doesn't seem like your speed." She paused her flirtations to curl her lip upward in disgust as she waved her hand around in general. There's a story there but I really don't care.

"Here on business, you sound like you don't care for the place, so why are you here?"

I guess she took that as an invitation as she plops down next to me, further hiking up the flimsy material of her dress. "I'm leaving this hell hole tomorrow. I've had nothing but bad luck so I'm going to explore the world or any place that isn't here. Besides, nothing to keep me here except vicious rumors and lies. I'm celebrating my departure and looking for some company? You interested in some...fun?"

Her fingertips traced my arm and made their way to my upper thigh before I stopped her inches shy of palming me. I don't jump to the sudden intrusion because I knew she would try but I look at her and shake my head.

"No thanks pretty lady, I'm on a mission to find my mate and she's in this town. It wouldn't be fair to her if I go sleeping with anyone."

She is practically in my lap; her lips graze my ear. "You know, she doesn't have to know. I'm known to have a man in bliss in no time. The tricks I know…" She trails off and kisses my ear. Kas roars forward, catching me off guard.

Shit!

"I said no. Mate here and that not you, move on slut." My Alpha voice booms as he growls. Well, there goes my cover...

I blink and I'm back, but she had clamored away in fear. Perhaps that wasn't the best course because now everyone is looking at me. Oh well, I chuckle and go back to enjoying the music and my beer. The guys join occasionally throughout the night, but I know what will happen.

It's 2 a.m. when we return and everyone has a guest except me, and my walls are not as thick as I need them to be right now. Even listening riles me up, but I try to calm my breathing and will myself to sleep. I'm about to doze off until...

"There! Right there...oh, don't stop!"

I growl and slam a pillow over my head.

Why couldn't I have met her tonight then I'd be making them jealous while sealing my permanent bond with her.

I shove my noise canceling headphones in, hoping that feature wasn't a gimmick.

I woke up envious and even more determined. Fitz links me he was cooking breakfast to make up for last nights after hour activities. I hear them bragging as I come down the stairs.

"Morning Chris, I cooked a bit of everything. You have got to hear what these two horndogs did last night. Go on, tell him what you did! Never mind, I'll tell you, they let them swap! Did you do that sneaky twin shit and switch in the bathroom or something?"

Kirin and Kellan look at each other and shake their heads. As twins they always get these questions. "Nah, we were honest and said if they wanted, they could have us both. They whispered to each other then agreed. It was...the best!" They quickly high-fived, "Hey, we should call them over tonight, I don't know about you, but I could have another go. What about you, Fitzy? I heard the way that girl was screaming for you last night..."

Fitz plates another round of bacon as I pour a glass of orange juice. "Yeah, she was good but I'm not...I don't know. I'm okay with not seeing her again."

I raise my brow, "Could it be...my Beta is contemplating the importance of his mate? Eventually, you'll feel that tug, you all will. Now, I've got a mission to complete."

He ignores my question, "Well, we got the rest of the day to look around, so you have any idea where you want to start?"

"Yeah, where women always go, the mall and there were two shopping centers, too. Liquid gold. I should get dressed."

"Let me guess, something black." They all laugh, and I sarcastically join in.

"A ha ha ha, whatever. No one's complained yet. Be ready in 45 minutes." I raise my brow before heading upstairs.

I choose a plain black shirt and dark wash jeans with my boots. I pull my locs back to complete the bad boy persona.

Wandering around Lovenshire, this is the epitome of a small town. There are no big chain restaurants, no museums, not even an IMAX theater, even we have one of those. It reminds me of that old show, Twin Peaks. All I need is a moose casually crossing the street or drinking from a stream. Though that might freak me out.

The mall is a decent size and an epicenter for crowd gatherings. We walk around after a stop at a Pretzel Barn and Kas is scanning but not picking up on her scent. I see a lot of wandering eyes from the passing groups of women whispering to each other but with my hearing, I'm well aware of their naughty talk whether they be wolf or human. You'd be surprised how many want to be tied up and spanked, even had a few with a daddy kink. In my wilder days, I'd be all over that.

It's almost 3 p.m. by the time we leave the mall and head to the shopping center. We start at the candle shop and my nose is assaulted by the scent of cinnamon, nutmeg, and pumpkin. It smells like Thanksgiving. I find something more masculine, leather and cigars, and buy a few for the house.

After a few more stores my stomach growled or it may have been Kas, either way, it was time for food. We spot a sandwich shop across the street and walk over there.

We're chatting about hosting a bike rally back home. As we round the corner, I notice someone in my path, so I sidestep to not plow into them. That's when I lock eyes on a woman and she's happily dancing around outside of an art shop, I think. She seemed excited about something but there was something else that caught my senses...her scent! That intoxicating unmistakable combination of cinnamon and an ocean breeze. We lock eyes, I smile, and she freezes momentarily then gives a quick smile before returning her focus back to whatever is going on in the studio.

Kas is howling in my damn ear.

K: That's her! Mate! Found mate, talk to her! Take her! Mark her, claim her, now!

Before I could respond to Kas' demand, I watch her open the door and nod at the same time Miller walked out. I turned around and walked away quicker, hoping he didn't spot me. She's in his pack with that subtle gesture instead of a bow.

We make it to the sandwich shop, order, and once settled down I reveal the news, "I saw her, it was the redhead dancing outside of the art studio, her scent confirmed it. Kas is losing his mind after spotting her. Now I know what my beautiful girl looks like."

All their mouths fall open in shock, "What?! Why didn't you say anything when you realized it? We should go back!"

"Miller was coming out of the studio she was going into; I didn't feel like having an audience. Besides it's a small town, I'll run into her again. She was perfectly beautiful." I eat while imagining how I'll act the next time I run into her. She looked like she was a spitfire, all it took was gazing into her eyes if even for a moment.

I stayed in that night while they went back out to Jack's. I expected them to come back with company, perhaps the same girls from the last time but was pleasantly surprised to see them come back empty-handed.

Fitz knew what I was saying without a single word said and he shrugs his shoulders, "It was a quiet night besides we wanted a couple of drinks. And we need to be level-headed for the search tomorrow, besides we wanted to see if we saw her there tonight, but she wasn't there. Thank goddess she has that siren red hair to make searching easier."

I zoned out thinking about wrapping those fiery locks around my hand as I pull her into an intense lip lock, taking her breath away. That night, I continued my deliciously sinful fantasy about my siren. It was so vivid, like I was there, listening to her call my name and hearing her gasp. "Christian" she'd moan so effortlessly. Her skin like cashmere and her lips like honey. I woke up panting then I laid there trying to will my erection down and to calm my racing heart. I need to find her soon because that urge would not go away.

It's been two days and I haven't spotted her once; I worry that maybe she was here on business and had already left. But Kas assured me he could smell faint traces of her around town. This morning we hit this diner that everyone was raving about and after the grueling two-hour workout, I was ready to chow down, within reason.

We arrive at the diner and a slightly older waitress tells us to take the booth at the far end. She comes back with water and takes our orders before working her section on the other side. Apparently, it was a busy day to visit as most tables were full. We got the last table that would fit us all.

"Well, we've been here almost four days, Chris and we've got nothing. Now what? I don't want to sound negative..."

I cut him off, "Don't worry Fitzy, I can't get this close and not keep going. We're close, I can feel it. As a matter of fact," My senses flared before I could finish, a waitress came out from the kitchen with a tray full of food, her auburn curls fell perfectly around her angelic face. She's even more beautiful up close and she works here! My eyes glow gold as she repeats our order, but she hasn't looked up as she balances our plates.

"Alright, I have three double cheeseburger platters all medium rare with fries. A Philly cheesesteak with fries and a chicken wrap with a Caesar side salad." A giggle slips her lips knocking Kas out of control and I gain it back as I shift myself and raise my brow.

"What's funny about my order?" Her beautiful smile fades when she looks at me and I feel a little bad. Did I look upset, or did she think I would complain about her behavior? I would never put her job in jeopardy but now she looks embarrassed. She finally regains her composure and clears her throat, "It's just different than all the carnivores at the table, is all. You guys enjoy your meal and let me know if you need anything else." My heart is racing as she turns to walk away. Everyone grabs their plate, pulling them closer, while the twins split the Philly cheesesteak. They were lucky enough to have that high metabolism.

I sigh loudly, "Sweet Moon Goddess what is she doing to me? She's perfect, absolutely perfect."

Kirin digs into his food, Kellan follows but Fitz claps my back, "She's going to make our pack that much stronger. What's the next step?"

I had several options including walking back into that kitchen and taking her lips, but I had to feel her out. "I'll leave my number in the tip and she'll call. Did you see her blushing when I spoke up? I saw every goosebump on her arms, she's curious." I neglected to mention I could smell the sweet scent of her arousal.

The food was delicious, we headed back to the house and chill out. I pay the bill and fold my note to her into the gracious tip and hope for the best.

I can see her in the kitchen from a window and she's trying to calm her breathing, I laugh to see my effect on her. I had high hopes, but I'd be lying if I didn't have doubt. Not all wolves believe in mates, or they reject them to live a carefree life. I hoped she still believed in the tradition.

I got my answer when I was barely through the front door and my phone buzzed.

N: Hi, this is Nessa, the waitress from earlier.

My heart was pounding, I was nervous. I realized I was standing in the foyer while everyone had walked around me heading to the kitchen and living room. I hear the TV startup, almost distracting me.

C: I was hoping to hear from you, beautiful. How about I take you out sometime?

There. I laid it out on the line, no going back now. My phone buzzes and I look down.

N: Listen, I have to be honest, I haven't had the best luck with men lately, so I need to ask, are you married? Kids? Notorious serial killer? I'm honestly tired of the lies.

I was stunned, what had my poor sunflower been through? Obviously, she's still not connected the dots to me being her mate, or she's feeling me out, so I take it slow.

C: O...kay but no to all your questions and you see, you just hadn't met me yet. I consider myself quite the prize.

Wow, I sound like a colossal douchebag, and I was only meaning to make her laugh I hope she took it as a joke.

Jeez, pull yourself together, Chris.

I go into the kitchen, grab a beer, and sit at the island. I hear them cheer. I assume they found a game to watch.

Bzzzz

N: *Oh yeah, then why aren't you snatched up yet? Mr. Quite the prize...*

She's feisty and I love it. I feel the chemistry brewing. Even over the phone, everything about her seems perfect. I'm not looking for a submissive partner, maybe sometimes, and only in the bedroom. No, I need her to keep me in line and not be afraid to challenge me, respectfully. She needed to be as fiery as her hair color.

I realized I was daydreaming and quickly typed my response.

C: *Because you haven't met me yet, so what do you say? Dinner?*

I exhaled the breath I didn't even know I was holding. I set my phone down to tap my fingers nervously as I waited for those three dots to indicate she was typing. My stomach was in knots as I checked the time, it felt like 15 minutes. I looked at the time on my message, it's been two minutes. She's either thinking about her options or trying to let me down easily. This makes me more anxious, and I have to dissipate this energy. I pace the floor, totally in my own thoughts.

She's going to say no.

She's probably dating some rich powerful wolf and is falling for his charming ways.

No, she said she had been hurt.

She's seeing if she can trust you enough to try again.

Please, my sweet girl, give me a chance, I...

My phone buzzes and I hurry back to read her response.

N: Sure, why not...when?

"Yes!!!" I scream out my excitement, I got my date with my dream girl.

C: I'll let you know...take care, gorgeous.

I celebrated while pouring myself a stiff shot, my nerves were bad, but I got my date!

"What happened? Did she answer your fifth-grade love note?" I tip my shot back; it burns so good.

"Well, are you going to tell me what happened or what?!" Fitz follows me out to the living room, no need to say it more than once.

"Hey, she responded to lover boy's message." He joked and the twins chuckled, but then everyone focuses on me to continue the story.

"She agreed to a date."

"Sweet! So, when is it? If it's tonight you need to get ready, you look rough."

"No, I haven't set a date, yet. I know this is going to sound crazy, but I should get back to the pack, we've been gone for almost a week. I will let her know I have some business to attend to before we go on our date."

"What?! The pack is fine Chris, I've been getting updates daily. We can afford another day or two, or you can stay back, and we'll go."

I shake my head, "I have a plan to build up our conversation over the phone, establish a pattern of sweet messages so she can be excited for our inevitable date. Besides, the yearly assessments are in three days, and you know how important that is to the longevity of the pack. We need to assess every single available warrior and assign additional training if they are not up to par. That itself is going to take at least a week."

He scoffs at me, "She's going to be married by the time you return."

"Don't worry, her only knight in shining armor is me. Let's pack and head out tonight."

I sent her a message letting her know I had some business to attend to, but after that she would be my priority, to come back and sweep her off her feet. She replies with a simple "Okay", but she didn't know how much I planned to romance her while I was gone.

The assessments were more brutal than anticipated, especially for my security detail, it was painfully obvious that they would not be ready for a sudden attack, and I was highly disappointed. After the last person of my security completed and failed their test, I called for an immediate six-mile run and two-hour combat session. Just because we were at peace did not mean we could slack. It was highly unacceptable.

They were put onto a new routine until they showed improvement. I would participate, so it didn't seem like punishment, but it was.

After dealing with that disaster, I left my beauty a voicemail expressing that I couldn't stop thinking about her, how stunning I thought she was, and that I couldn't wait for our date. She replied with a thank you and a smiley face.

It was an upgrade from the 'okay' I received at first.

It took about a week to evaluate every single body in the pack, and I was exhausted but that didn't hinder me from sending my good morning and good night texts. Her responses became longer and sweeter, she would wish me well in what I was doing and that my texts make her smile. I was weaving a delicate pattern of trust and to show her she had obviously been dealing with the wrong guys.

From what I could piece together she was a party girl. Not a sloppy, falling in the bushes type drunk, but she enjoyed being the center of attention. She seemed like she would dance on top of the table or bar, seducing me with her slow sultry movements, rolling her hips and swaying side to side, her intense gaze never leaving mine as she captured my attention.

Shit. I look down to a big problem. *I need to take care of this.* She doesn't even know how badly she is affecting me, but she will.

I was lost in the thought of her when I get a message from security on the secret link, it was only used for emergencies.

"Echo Bravo, this is an echo bravo transmission. Alpha there are reports of unauthorized movement in the archives."

You have to be kidding me! He doesn't learn, does he? Well, I'll make sure the message gets to him loud and fucking clear!

"Have security posted outside the main doors and leadership at the back and the secret access tunnel."

"Yes, Alpha. That's where they came in."

I felt my anger reaching the tipping point, only pack members knew about the tunnels throughout the grounds. This was an inside job, and I was about to rip this person in two. Maybe I jumped the gun blaming Damien.

"No one approach, I will handle the traitor."

"You think it's a pack member?" Kirin asked, I knew everyone was thinking the same, but he asked first.

"Who else would know about the tunnel access? If they aren't part of the pack, they got the information from the inside." I say as I come from the house to the archives building. Fitz, Kirin, and Kellan were awaiting orders. Kirin and Kellan already in their wolves if there was more than one or they tried to escape. Both were huge honey blonde wolves with black as night eyes, even during the night they were intimidating.

I hadn't changed from my pajamas; I was still in my black silk pants and no shirt. If I needed to shift, I wouldn't care about ripping these to shreds.

"They still in there?" I confirm with the head of my security detail.

"Yes Alpha, we have eyes on them. They look to be taking photos from one of the history books and the display cases about your family."

I wouldn't hear another word, I needed to get answers to why they would betray me or the pack! Kas is ready to shift and splatter their blood all over the walls, but I held him back. Tavi was watching from the sidelines as he was immersed in an ancient-looking book. I was beginning to believe I couldn't count on him when the time came. He should stand side by side with Kas ready to deal out the punishment but instead, he's sitting on the side reading a book.

T: You don't want to confirm your Legacy status to them with a grand reveal. I'm monitoring the situation from the back. Kas has control.

Hmmm, how nonchalant, but he's right.

I signal through the camera to our team in the tower to turn off the alarm, so I don't trigger it. I tell Fitz to stay by this door as I slide through. My hearing is impeccable as I hear the shutter click of pictures being taken. They're even dumb enough to use the flash, what if security was walking by? But it's so much worse with the subject of their snooping right behind them. As I get closer, I hear talking but not sure if there is more than one person. I remain silent for a moment.

"He's going to pay for what he did to me! I am going to enjoy bringing him to his knees!" I peek around the corner to see Bambi flipping pages and taking pictures. That sneaky, conniving slut!

"I could have made him happy! I would make an amazing Luna to this worthless pack but I'm not his *mate,*" Her tone was condescending, "what can she do that I can't?"

"Well, for one, she wouldn't do something so traitorous." I come around the corner and her eyes go wide with shock.

"Chrissy! I..."

I growl, "I've told you incessantly not to fucking call me that! Did you really think you could get away with this? Betraying your pack, your Alpha?! Unless...I'm not really YOUR Alpha...Who are you working for?"

She went from looking shocked to looking confident in her mischief. A loud sinister laugh spills from her lips and then this inhumane scream. "You're such an ignorant fool! You could have made me your Luna and we could have doubled our pack instantly. But now, my uncle will wage war against you once he has proof of what you are, and I'll be so grateful to help him bring you down. He's a visionary, you Alphas are too stuck in your archaic rules!"

"I won't ask you again...who sent you?" By now her speech perked Tavi's interest.

"Didn't you ever wonder where my family was or why I was alone? Giving that sad sap story of my family dying in a fire like 100 miles away? There was indeed a family that tragically died and I used that to get in. I'm a rogue, a damn good rogue, covering it up with a magic potion! I was right on top of you, but you were too worried about getting your dick sucked! Believe me, I was hesitant the first few times but once I realized how stupid you were I basked in being...right under your nose. For a mythical creature specially made by the Moon Goddess herself, you're none too bright." She leans cockily against the glass case tossing the camera up and catching it, basking in her grand reveal.

"So, you give your uncle this alleged proof, what's in it for you?"

"The title I deserve! I will be his pack's Luna! They will bow to me and soon... you will, too."

Kas is growling at the revelation, he's begging me to let him take over.

Not yet, Kas. Just a little more.

"Who is this high and mighty Alpha who sent his "Luna" instead of manning up and coming here himself? He must not give a damn about you returning because no one ever comes back...ever. Or did he not reveal that little tidbit of information? Nope, we ripped them to shreds before tossing their carcasses into the ocean. every trespasser." I grin as her eyes went wide, "I'm assuming this man you speak of is Damien because only he would do some dumb shit like this. Did I hit the nail on the head, hmm? I bet he didn't relay my latest threat to him that if he breached my compound again that I would send a treaty drenched in their blood declaring war. Did you know that, huh? The fact that you want to be a Luna for your uncle is sick and shows how screwed up you are in the head." I felt the glow before I saw it and she did too. "I knew it! I knew you were a Legacy; he was right!" I couldn't deny it, but I wasn't planning on showing her either. Tavi had taken it upon himself. I lean forward and I see her flinch, hesitant about how dangerous I might be. "Don't worry, you won't live long enough to disclose that bit of information. I'm going to make sure that Damien gets my message loud and clear when I sign the war declaration and drench it in your blood! Guards!"

They rush in and take her into custody and the camera drops from her hands. I pick it up and crush it, destroying all she was going to leak to Damien. I was stunned, she had been in our pack for almost two years, and she immediately set her sights on me; now I know why. A mole in my pack, I seriously underestimated Damien, but so did she. She didn't realize he was sacrificing her for his own gain.

"Take her to the dungeon and get all the details. I'll finish the job afterward."

"How extreme do you want to go, sir?"

I look Bambi dead in the eyes as my eyes turn gold and Kas roars forward. "By any means necessary." I clear my throat and take control, "You heard him; she's like any other traitor."

"No, Chris, please! Didn't we have fun together, I made a mistake! Don't do this! I won't tell him anything, I won't tell him what I saw, please!" She clasps her hands together, begging for my mercy.

She won't get it. Then I give her some interesting news for her to ponder before she dies.

"Oh, I thought you'd like to know, I found my Luna. It won't be too long before she takes her rightful place beside me on the throne. A queen for her king..."

I smirk as I see the jealousy and envy in her eyes.

"But you won't live long enough to meet her. You'll be lucky to make it until morning. Take her away!"

Kas is hopping around in my head, happy that I brought up our mate and now I can't get her out of my head, not that I want to. I check my watch. It's late, but I have to see if she's still up.

I make my way back to my room, lying down in bed, rubbing my stomach with my hand. Not to sound cocky, but my abs were ripped, I pride myself on looking good naked.

"Hello. Christian?" Her soft scratchy voice knocks me out of my thoughts.

"Yeah, it's me. Were you sleeping? I'm sorry I needed to hear your voice. It was a bad day here."

She yawns, "It's okay, I want to talk. What happened, are you okay?"

"I'm fine now that I'm talking to you. How was your day?"

"Chris, this isn't about me. You called me."

"Yes, but hearing about you makes me feel better. How was work?"

She concedes, "Kind of busy but in a good way, made a killing in tips. It helps to flirt a bit; that's how I got your number."

She'll never have to work for tips again when she's my queen. She can have everything her heart desires.

"True, hope you didn't get any more numbers. If I remember correctly, I still owe you a date."

"Yes, you do! When are you coming back? You got me excited then you had to go on business. It's been two weeks…" She drew out the word weeks for emphasis.

"Soon, beautiful, very soon. I promise it's worth the wait. Get some sleep and thanks for talking away my bad day. Sweet dreams."

"Sweet dreams, Chris." I hear what sounds like a kiss before she hangs up. That little gesture sealed the deal. I'm going back to Lovenshire tomorrow and surprise her. I can't wait to bask in her scent.

I had one piece of unattended business before I went to sleep.

C: Kas, where is Tavi?

T: Don't ask that mutt. I can speak for myself.

C: Oh, then why would you reveal yourself to her?! Don't forget I'm in charge here, not you!

T: That traitor whore will die anyway, I thought I'd ease her mind.

C: What is your deal? That is not your decision to make!

T: You don't seem to be making any good ones since your father left you the pack.

C: What's that supposed to mean?

There's a long silent pause.

T: I apologize, master. I'll be in my corner, reading up on spells we should take advantage of.

And he walks away into the darkness.

K: Told you he's not right.

C: What did he mean about my decisions since my father died?

Kas shrugs and circles before plopping down to rest and suddenly I felt the exhaustion, too, but I was also excited to go surprise her. I can't help to think that Tavi reminds me of my father.

I go on my own back to Lovenshire, after the many failures and discovering Bambi's true intentions, I put the grounds on full lockdown and 12-hour shifts until I feel some semblance of safety. I don't leave pack grounds until after 6 p.m. to make sure all my protocols are intact. I want updates every 12 hours until further notice.

I'm mildly irritated, I wanted to spend the day with her, but I'll do even better and take her to dinner tomorrow. Besides, I believe she's working an extended shift today, but I would've spent the entire day at the diner with her.

I arrived at the hotel, settled into my deluxe King suite, ordered room service, then took a hot shower before changing into my boxers. I was only staying the night; I'd go to my place in the morning. There was no food at my house, and I forgot to order some for delivery but I'm having them delivered tomorrow. Tonight, the hotel feeds me.

I lay there and daydream about her and find my mind wandering towards mating. I fantasized about her smile and her full lips, how they would feel against every part of my body, how she filled out that uniform so deliciously, and as soon as my hand shifted south there was a knock, undoubtedly room service.

I decided to text her to know what she was doing and to finally confirm our date.

Poor thing just got off from work but she's so eager for our date tomorrow. If I was there, I'd give her an amazing massage to soothe those aching muscles and then...

I sigh and look to see that she sent me her address, but she was exhausted and going to bed. I wished her sweet dreams. Tomorrow I would sweep her off her feet.

After checking out, settling into my place, putting the food away, and then taking a nap, I spent most of the next day at the movie theater to pass the time.

Tonight's outfit is simple, a black Henley shirt and jeans and I add my favorite leather jacket, revealing my bad boy persona. I hopped in my rental and stopped by a small flower shop to grab a bouquet. It was an assortment of tulips and orchids.

I listen to some calming music in front of her apartment building to take the edge off, besides I'm early. She doesn't know how much power she holds over me already. I'm usually so confident but she makes me vulnerable. I chuckle to myself and wipe my face with my hand.

Time to grab the little lady.

I'm not impressed by the building or the lack of security as I head to the front entrance. I walked past the back exit being held open by a rock. I chucked it as far as I could. No way I would allow that. The front had an old school buzzer system and no cameras. She won't be living here once I establish our relationship. I hit the buzzer and she immediately let me in.

I find her door, take a deep breath before I knock. I hear shuffling and something sliding across the floor before the knob turns and I'm met by the sexiest sight.

That is the luckiest piece of fabric and I'm jealous. I take her and spin her, I have to get the full view because, besides her radiant smile, her ass is her second-best asset. To avoid locking her in her place and marking her I ask if she's ready. She says yes, turning back and bending over to grab a sweater.

Fuck me. Kas comes to the surface and growls just enough for her to hear. I pull him back into my subconscious.

She chuckles, "I guess I don't need to figure out if you're a werewolf or not, huh?"

I smirk at her, "What gave it away?"

She states the low growl was a dead giveaway and the eyes confirmed it.

C: *Could you have some tact? I got this, okay?!*

K: *Kas not sorry! Mate finally here, smell so good and so pretty.*

I roll my eyes as I escort her to the car. I noticed she was quiet. I asked if she was okay, she nodded, so I left her to her thoughts. I play some smooth R&B to set the mood.

I'm interrupted by her voice, "Christian, can I ask you a question that's not too forward?"

She could ask me to give her a million dollars and I would. I shift to face her, resting my arm around her headrest. I watch her breathing hitch and give her my sly smile. I swear to the Moon Goddess if she bites her lip, I will take her here and now.

She fidgets and asks about Kas because her wolf was curious. Naturally...

I see him puff out his chest as if he needs any more reason to be arrogant. She tells me her wolf's name is Dalila. Kas spent the next minute repeating it repeatedly, yipping and prancing about until I told him to knock it off so I could focus on driving.

We arrived at a stylish little bistro with a private area perfect for me to focus on her.

We park and she hasn't moved, "Hey darlin', we're here."
She blinks rapidly before setting her sights on the
restaurant and she gasps, "Christian, it's beautiful. But,
why here?"

She sounded like she didn't deserve to be wined and
dined or spoiled but she deserved that and so much
more. I reach behind her and grab the bouquet. Her eyes
light up and she blushes, thanking me quietly.

As we approach, I see the host is about to bow and I
shake my head to stop him. That's all I need is for him to
blow my cover as an Alpha before I'm able to tell her
and I can't have that. He greets and guides us to the
secluded area in the back. I tell him to let everyone know
not to acknowledge my status.

He motions to the table and stands by her seat, I dismiss
him. That's my job, not his. I seat her and surprise her
with a chaste kiss before sitting down.

We chat about random stuff to break the ice. I discover
she loves classic cars like I do, she even joked about
wanting to get a motorcycle. That would be a dream, her
and I riding side by side along the coastline until we find
a diner. We'd go to Sturgis for the annual rally, and I'd
convince her to have a quickie on my bike near the lake
or even a mountain view. I'd also enjoy the idea of her
holding on to me as we take the winding roads doing
80+ mph.

She tells me she also enjoys a good horror movie, anything with gratuitous violence and bloodshed, action movies being a close second.

And she eats when she's hungry. She doesn't do that 'cute eating with a salad', she loves nachos, tacos, and loves to cook and learn new recipes. That's why she's curvy in all the right places.

I could listen to her talk until the morning, but the restaurant closes at 11 p.m. I'm nervous but I reach for her hand.

When I finally said we had to talk I could see her brain trying to figure out where I was going with this. Her fences were going up almost as an immediate response.

I kiss her hand before I blurt it out, "Nessa, you're... my mate, my beautiful girl who makes my heart pound and my stomach fill with butterflies. Kas has been buzzing in my ear ever since he saw you and I have been trying to ignore him, but the more I talk to you, the more intrigued I become, and I knew you were something special to me."

I see the range of emotions, shock, fear, and some confusion and maybe even realization of what I am saying. I squeeze her hand to show she's not dreaming. I am confessing my adoration for her. She's still silent so I continue, "I was content with being the lone rebel who didn't need anything or anyone until I met your gorgeous eyes outside that studio, I couldn't wait to see you again. I was so lucky to go to the diner and find you working there. I guess the Moon Goddess kept putting me in your path for a reason and I am glad she chose someone beautiful, smart, and kind as you. I can tell you've been fighting these feelings too and I want you to know we can take it slow; you don't have to say anything, know that I'm already in love with you, Vanessa."

I said it. I told her I loved her and I do.

When she's around I feel complete, I feel it over our phone conversations and text messages, there's no doubt in my mind, she's my one. When I brush her cheek lightly, I see the exact moment when she finally feels our attraction, the sparks and tingles move between us, and we enjoy the feeling while her face lights up in laughter.

I hold her chin and lean forward placing my lips to hers. She tastes like honey, and I want more... I pull back and smirk. "I've been dying to kiss you since I met you. I can't wait to mark you and make you mine."

She leans forward more, crossing her legs, that sexy dress moving further up her thigh. I'm jolted out of my fantasy when her hand lands on my upper thigh. I swear I shot up so fast and she raises a brow.

"Then let's go." She leans forward and I wait for her lips to be on mine, but she backs away before we connect with a mischievous, sexy grin. She gets up and saunters away putting an extra sway to her hips.

Fuck, that did it.

I drop some money and follow her, catching up, I pin her against the door. I need to touch her, to feel her under me, to taste her.

It takes the strength of many moons to pry me off her to make the drive back home. We arrive in record time. She removes her heels at the door and walks curiously towards the kitchen then back and up the stairs. She stands in the hallway at the top of the stairs, so I come up behind her, holding her tight, nuzzling her neck, enjoying her scent.

"There are three guest bedrooms and a bathroom that way and of course my room over here." I tell her while still hugging her, I walk us to the double doors. She opens them and at that moment I realize I hadn't tidied up.

Dammit! My bed is a mess. I assure her that I'm not some filthy slob and she laughs wandering toward my bookshelf.

Although a vacation property, I made sure that it held some of my staples from home to include a small collection of books. She perused the shelf and her eyes lit up at my selection, I even held her all-time favorite. I assured her that proved that she was meant for me.

I lead her to the bathroom and tease her about using the shower later and I already know what positions I want her in underneath the stream of the rainforest shower.

She pulls me out of my thoughts and into the middle of the bedroom, I trace my lips along her neck, and I feel her shudder. I nip the hollow space and she moans. That sweet sound riles both me and Kas. If she continues, I won't be able to keep Kas down. She turns away and lets her dress fall to her feet. I followed the falling fabric until my eyes made their way back upward.

She's practically spilling out of her bra, it's a rose gold colored set. Her hands wander her curves as she moans and then...bites her lip.

Kas roars forward as he attacks her with kisses, caressing her, making her pant. All the commotion brings out her wolf, Dalila as they claw at each other. Kas tosses her on the bed and Nessa gains control back from Dalila as her sexy voice begs me, "Mmm, please."

I strip down so quickly I forgot that this is her first time seeing me naked. Judging by the look on her face, as I'm climbing on the bed, she's a bit shocked. She doesn't look as confident as she did earlier.

I reassure her, "Don't worry, love, it'll be a perfect fit...but first I want my lips on yours..." I kissed her inner thigh, teasing her and taking the time to drive her crazy until I'm finally tasting what's mine. She claims her first orgasm quickly, then I flip her on her stomach kissing my way up her back, her delicate skin so deliciously fragrant she purrs under me.

"Mark me, Christian. Make me yours and only yours. I've never wanted someone as much as I want you... I need you."

Those words light a fire within me as she gives me permission to finally claim her body as mine. I wrap her auburn hair around my hand and pull, exposing her neck, "Gladly, I'm yours and you're mine."

My canines extend as I clamp down hard and fast and she screams out momentarily. She was not prepared for that, but an Alpha mark is more aggressive and deeper, it's how we were taught. I look at her and she is not happy. She's still yelling at me until she pauses abruptly…

She goes quiet and I smile smugly. The mark is showing, and it looks perfect against her dewy skin.

I could see her brain trying to put two and two together then she inhales and shuts her mouth then opens it again, "H-have you met Alpha Miller?" She questions me and I know she's trying to confirm but not flat out ask. I shift to my side and fix the sheets.

"Always, anytime I visit another pack's land I always pay my respects to the Alpha..." She was so confused because I owned property here, but I explained that I had made a deal with Alpha Miller to obtain it.

I can see the wheels coming to a screeching halt as she finally asks, "Who are you?" I couldn't help the smile that forms, it was time to reveal everything. I take her hand and kiss it.

"Christian Grey, Alpha of the elusive and mysterious Midnight Shadow Pack. But more importantly, is who YOU are going to be. You, my dear, are soon to be Vanessa Grey, Luna to said pack."

She was obviously surprised but then she smiled as she straddled me. "Do I get to mark the big...bad Alpha as he marked me? I want everyone to know that you're mine, too." I don't know why but that made me even harder to know she wanted to claim her Alpha. It's not required but she asked me with so much lust in her voice, I wouldn't deny her. I give her the go and she sank her teeth in and immediately I had the urge to slam her against the wall and already try to extend our family. Instead, we enjoy a romp in the shower and a dip in the hot tub before our first night together.

I'm standing in the same building at the Cheshire Pack. I'm already inside and I am thumbing through a huge leather-bound book with illustrations of the family tree. What am I even looking for? I realize that a sinister laugh is coming from me, but I am not laughing. I feel like I am watching from behind a mirror, watching someone take my body over and break into the compound, back into this building...looking.... searching...but what for?

And then there was a flash and I was back in my office with my crew. "Leave no survivors, burn it all to the ground so the other packs know not to ever think about attacking us, the most powerful pack in the world! It is our destiny! My father said it would be so...by any means." I let out a vicious roar and my crew responds in equally animalistic howls.

Then there's a flash of battle and I see myself walking out the burning remains of Alpha Miller's place with his still-beating heart in my hand and his severed head in the other.

I shot up from bed so fast, I almost fell from it. I went into the bathroom so as not to disturb Nessa. I am surprised I did not wake her from the movement. I leaned against the countertop looking into my reflection.

C: Kas, where is Tavi?

K: Witch not here, he gone again.

C: What the fuck, how is he able to separate himself from me and me not notice? Something is wrong Kas, I don't know what to do. I don't know if there is anything I can do but I need to find out. I can't keep having these visions of destroying other packs. It's like my father's still trying to complete his plan of becoming the supreme pack.

K: Need to talk to stupid witch to see what he up to. Not comfortable in own space, think he wants to hurt Kas.

C: You let me know the next time he comes around we need to settle this ASAP. I can risk no danger to her.

K: Got it.

I exhaled loud and long, frustration muddling my perfect night, the night I claimed my mate. This was supposed to be a no-brainer fantastic night but now my stomach is in knots.

Something is brewing and I fear...I may cause it.

I, once again, try to focus on the beauty in front of me. Messy hair strewn all over the pillowcase and little snores escape her lips. She whined, indicating she was missing my touch. I climbed back into bed and licked her mark before kissing it. She moans and then sighs before bumping her ass against me causing a stir. I hear her giggle, she's not asleep and for that, I keep her up for the rest of the night.

The next morning, we talked about the pack, where it's located, and how I couldn't wait to show her the packhouse and end the first day there watching the sunset over the pristine cliffs and listening to the crashing of the waves.

I feel relieved knowing I wouldn't have to convince her to come with me, that she was eager to start our journey together. She was fawning over Kayd's relationship with Kam and she wanted what her best friend had. She was over the party scene and ready to settle down roughly around the same time I had thought the same thing.

"So, Luna Kamari is your best friend? Well, how fitting, she can help you adjust but I already know you're going to be an amazing Luna. I want to take things slow; we can talk about moving and quitting your job, you don't have to work another day in your life."

She snuggles up to me and sighs. She requests one thing before agreeing to come back with me. She looks in my eyes and gazes into my soul, I feel the warmth in my heart. She wants one last night of partying in town before she starts chapter one of our lives together. What's the harm? I get to see her celebrate the end of her time here and then whisk her away to our happy ever after.

But first, I reach into the dresser, "Only if you promise to wear this so they know that this party girl is spoken for."

I know it sounds crazy to already have purchased an engagement ring but from our talks I felt I made a great choice; it was a rose gold diamond matching the underwear she was wearing earlier.

Mental reminder to self to replace the set that now lay in pieces on the bedroom floor.

Her mouth falls open then she raises her brow, "You just happen to have an engagement ring with you?"

Okay, it seems odd, but I knew what I wanted the end game to be. I confidently bought what I thought would be the perfect ring for her. Now her face softens and I wait patiently for her answer.

Her smile becomes a mile wide, "...yes, I would love to be the future Mrs. Christian Grey and Luna of the Midnight Shadow pack!"

I know I heard her say it, but I still couldn't believe it. I slip on the ring as she cries happily.

A little later I realize a tough discussion needs to be had because I need to return to the pack tonight or early tomorrow. The updates have been consistent, and all seems back to normal, but I need to see for myself. Me not being there leaves them vulnerable and I can't risk it.

I smell something amazing coming from the kitchen as I come down in my grey sweats, one of the few non-black items I own. I see her at the stove tossing pasta in a fragrant creamy red sauce. I spin her quickly and return the sweet kiss she gave me earlier.

"Mmm, well I'll cook all the time to get a kiss like that. You want truffles on your pasta?"

"Please." And she quickly sprinkles it in before plating it. She grabs the sparkling water for her and a beer for me and sets them on the island. We sat next to each other.

"Darlin', I hate to bring this up after such an amazing night, but I'll need to return to my...*our* pack. There was a breach before I came here and they've been on restriction and a very strenuous regimen and as much as I'd like to stay and be under you night and day..."

She cuts me off with a kiss. "I understand...you have a whole pack of people you need to take care of. I'll be fine until your return. Besides, I liked getting spoiled by your text messages. Just know your fiancée will be here waiting for you. Go be great and I'll...I don't know, I guess I'll work to keep busy. I know I don't have to, but I can't mill around my place. Kam and Kayd are so in love it's insufferable, so pack grounds are off-limits."

I open a kitchen drawer and retrieve a key. I hold it up before handing it to her, "When you're ready. Besides, I'm not confident in the security of your current apartment, at least here it has 360-degree coverage and cameras."

"Chris..."

I tutted, "No argument, take your time but I want you fully settled in here upon my return, deal?"

She blushes and her eyes shut when I place a kiss on her forehead. She sighs and her whole body relaxes, "Okay, deal."

"Let's go out to a movie and maybe dinner, then I'll head back."

"You booked the flight already?" I saw the disappointment on her face, but I countered with a smile. "I own a private jet, sweetheart. A perk of being an Alpha."

"Ooh, nice. Can't wait to take advantage of that...and the mile-high club." She winks and I growl. "Easy, I can scrap all plans and take you now."

She yelps and grabs our plates to take to the sink. "You get one more round before you leave, better make the best of it. I'm going to get dressed." She winks.

She's crazy if she thinks I'm only taking her once, I have a two-time minimum; she just doesn't know it yet.

I brought a change of clothes as we got ready at her place. At the theater, we found a cheesy slasher flick. Watching her yell and scream at the screen like any advice would help the doomed characters is way more entertaining than the movie. It was another thing I loved about her; I knew she would be that steady hand I need for difficult decisions. I see her standing next to me, side by side, as we command our pack.

She nudges me out of my thoughts as the credits roll on the screen, "Let's go to the diner, I'll treat you to the secret menu."

And she did, she ordered the mac & cheeseburger and sweet potato fries. I will need an intense workout after this, I feel myself falling asleep in the booth until she whispers in my ear about sex. Now I'm moving at the speed of light back to my place. She may have said one time, but I convinced her that three times and five orgasms is the magical goodbye number. I extended the rental contract on the car for another week and a half so she can have it if she wants to move some of her stuff in sooner. I drive us to the airport, hop out with my bag, and hand it over to my steward. I turn back and she's pouting.

"Hey, come here."

She walks into my embrace. "I never knew I could miss someone so much and you haven't even left yet."

I kiss her forehead, "I already miss you, too. I'll let you know when I arrive, and you let me know when you're in the house and the alarm is on."

"Okay. Chris?"

I tilt her chin up and kiss her, "I love you, too, darlin'. Talk to you in a while."

I pull her in tighter. Then, there's a sniffle. "See you soon, *Mrs.* Grey." That caused a smile. "Okay, Mr. Grey, come back soon." The sparks flew as I gave her one long everlasting kiss and quickly boarded. She waved and then drove away before I taxied.

During the flight, I tried to sleep but I was back to being wound up about the pack and the discrepancies in security. Another wandering thought was why was I having all these dreams or warnings or whatever they were? I felt my phone buzz as I got a text from her.

N: *I'm back at my place to grab some clothes then I'll be in our bed thinking about you.*

Now that she's in my forefront my imagination wanders. I doze off the last hour and dream of her.

When the sedan pulls up to the front doors, I link my leadership to my office now. I walk forward, toward my desk, without a word and I can see how tense I made it. I laugh which breaks the tension, but they still wait for instruction. "Fellas please, sit. I want to thank you for monitoring the pack while I was away and instilling those harsh guidelines. I need our pack to be a cohesive unit especially when I introduce them to their Luna...and my fiancée."

"Whoa! She didn't think you were some creepy stalker who already had a ring? Hmm, guess I was wrong." Fitz shrugs his shoulders and I punch him in response.

"Yeah, you were wrong. My girl fell for me and now she's mine." I sigh, "But back to business, we can dial back the training from daily to three times a week effective immediately. Also, switch personnel around so they don't get complacent again. Maybe do 3 or 6-month rotations between the tower, the gate, and the dungeon. I need them to be alert and on their toes. We cannot let our guard down."

I know I sound paranoid, but Nessa was about to become a part of the pack and I needed to make sure she was safe. She, unfortunately, becomes a target because cowards always attempt to hurt the Alpha by hurting or even killing those closest to them.

I say this with no remorse, if any attempt is made on Vanessa, I'll make sure that the offending pack is wiped off this Earth and I'll burn their ashes and pack land to the ground!

It was at that moment I remember I needed to text Nessa; it was so late I wasn't even sure she was up. I dismiss them as I head towards my suite.

C: Hey, my beautiful girl, made it home, tended to some business, now going to bed. Sweet dreams, I'll buzz you in the morning.

I change and flop down on top of my sheets feeling myself fade into slumber until I hear a buzz.

N: Glad you're home, I'm all snug in your bed. It smells like you. I christened the sheets thinking about you. I hope that makes you dream of me. Love you, sweetheart. Night."

She's going to drive me crazy. I smile as my last thought before sleep is her sleeping in the sheets of our lovemaking, her self-love session with my name on her lips, and our scents mixed as one. I can't wait until I can smell her all over this house.

I'm startled at the crack of dawn when my pack sister comes banging at my door to start the remodel I requested. I wanted to rid all evidence of Bambi. I didn't think she'd start this early in the morning!

I answer the door angrily, but she brushes past me with a few movers to begin her vision. She shoos me into the bathroom knowing I needed to at least get dressed.

Twenty minutes later I'm out of the shower and in my towel brushing my teeth when my phone rings.

"Herro?" I tried to say hello, but I was mid-brush.

"Morning, what are you doing?"

I hear my angel and spit out the toothpaste. "Brushing my teeth, sorry, sweetheart. Good morning, beautiful. What are you doing?"

"I miss you. What's all that noise in the background, sounds like major construction!" She giggles as I hear Cameron barking orders.

"Close, I'm having my room remodeled for you today, so it'll be an elegantly designed love nest for us." She laughed; I didn't expect that reaction. "Yeah right, this is you cleansing your old indiscretions before I get there. That's a smart move. I should have done that when we went back to my place. Bet you were wondering who the last person in my bed was..."

A growl slipped thinking about it.

"Don't you start, you're literally erasing your tawdry history as we speak."

"It was not tawdry, just making a fresh start. Our pasts don't matter. Anyway, what are you planning on doing today?"

"Mmm, absolutely nothing. Going to lie in bed all day, completely naked."

I choked after I imagined her naked and tangled in the sheets. I hear her laughing. "That's not funny, how am I supposed to train and lead with that thought in my head?" She's quiet then my phone buzzes. I see a text has come in from her.

With an attachment.

Don't look, Christian. For the love of Moon Goddess don't look...

"I sent you something to help you, you're welcome."

I know I will regret it, but the temptation was too great. My phone lit up and I unlocked it to click on the attachment, "Holy shit. Darlin'..." I feel myself and Kas panting looking at a tastefully nude side view of her body. The black silk sheets covered enough to give me a peek of side boob and the curve of her ass. Her hair is slightly messy and covers part of her face with a seductive grin. Her full lips screamed to be kissed until she was gasping for air.

"The next time I get a hold of you, you're going to pay for sending me that."

"Mmm...looking forward to it. Now get to work Alpha, you have a long productive day ahead of you."

"We'll continue this later."

"Oh, I know. Much later. I love you, Chris."

"I love you, too, sunflower."

When I hang up, I hop back into the shower for a much-needed arctic blast. It does absolutely nothing to help but it was worth a shot. I come out and head to my closet trying not to disturb the workers.

"Hey, hurry up, we're not even close to being done. I gave you enough time to shower and get out. You're a distraction!" Cameron shouts at me while simultaneously shouting at her crew.

I grab some jeans and a shirt, "Alright, alright! Nessa will love you, you both boss me around with no consequences."

"Ooh, I like her already! By the way, did I hear you take two showers?" She raises her brow and I shake my head.

"Mind your business. Just make sure you're done as soon as possible. Thanks, little sis." I give her a quick kiss on the forehead and she screeches like a banshee while wiping her entire face. She hates public displays of affection...hey, I'm her big bro I'm supposed to embarrass her.

Cameron latched onto me when I took over, she was curious with all the responsibilities of an Alpha. She would ask a million questions and I grew to adore her like an annoying younger sibling. It was nice having some sort of family when I had no one else around.

Later, I gathered my pack on the training field. I could hear the grumbling, they thought I was subjecting them to yet another torturous training session, but I wasn't. I know they think I'm harsh but hopefully not cruel. I only care about their safety and the longevity of our pack. I am nothing without them and that's how I start my speech.

"Listen, without you I am nothing. It is all of you who make this pack great, not me. I am only here to guide and be the voice. I know it's been tougher since the breaches; I need to count on you to keep your pack family safe. I apologize for being so harsh, but I assure you that I will fight to my last breath for every one of you. But this is not about war or violence, I announce we are no longer on lockdown or 12-hour shifts."

The entire pack whooped and hollered in celebration. "And we will have a party that starts in a couple of hours to celebrate getting back to normal operations. Also, we will celebrate the fact that our Luna has been found." The gasps were even louder and the expressions ranged from joy to a few angry she-wolves who thought they had a chance or at least a shot at a one-night stand but they never did, Bambi ruined that.

"You will meet her soon. We are working on a few things in her hometown before she's a permanent fixture here. Her name is Vanessa Vanderbilt, she is from the Cheshire Pack, our neighbors to the East. I will make an announcement once we settle on her move-in date. That is all, please enjoy the festivities, you earned it!"

"Yes, Alpha!" They reply and disperse to get ready for the party. It'll be a pack picnic with lots of games and activities for the kids. Sometimes I forget that they suffer when I implement these strict rules, it keeps them inside.

I go to my office since they are still working on my suite, it does sound like major construction in there. I texted Nessa about announcing her arrival and the picnic to celebrate getting off restriction.

She calls me, "Hi handsome..."

"Hey sweetness, still naked?"

"Mmm, these silky sheets feel so good against my skin, but not as much as you do."

"Darlin'..." I'm one phone call from chartering my jet.

"I'll be good. I have been

wondering...are any of your past conquests part of the pack? Will I be a walking target for some jealous bitter bitch because I'll tell you this right now, I'm a scrapper. I am always prepared to fight. Kam can vouch for me."

"Not necessary, Nes. I had one steady person recently but...I got rid of her."

I thought I heard Kas growling at Tavi, but Tavi waved him off, mumbling something in Latin. I don't know fluent Latin but know a few words he spoke. Sounded like a spell, perhaps he's practicing.

"Hey sunflower, they should be gathering outside so I should go."

"O...kay. I have a shift today; I'll be off around 9 or 10 p.m."

"Don't work too hard. I'll call you before you go to bed."

"Mmm, promise to tuck...me...in?"

I didn't even have to see her face to know she had that look on her face, the one that screamed take me. "Definitely."

Our talk solidified my choice to go back next week so she can celebrate her final days in Lovenshire.

The day I would claim her, I woke up super grumpy. I can't be mad it's 5 a.m. because she'd be in my arms by 7:30 a.m.

Once landed, I hop in a rental heading thru town, I stop by the local florist for two dozen white orchids in a glass vase.

I felt my entire body electrify knowing I was only a few feet away at the front door. I had her answer the door rather than open it and go inside. I knock and for a moment I hear nothing, she is a heavy sleeper, so I knock a lot louder.

I hear her yelling as she comes closer, she swings the door open, "I swear, this better be the...what?!"

Her face went from fury to adoration when she saw the flowers I was hiding behind.

"Oh my gosh, these are so beautiful...but no card. Hmm, I bet they're from Michael, wait no Corey he loves spoiling me with things like this..."

I couldn't believe my ears! She was naming all these other guys but not me! Her fiancé!

I couldn't help the jealous growl and then she laughed.

"Babe, come on, I know it's you, your scent gives you away, remember? Thank you for the beautiful flowers, put them on the counter. I need to brush my teeth before greeting you properly."

She was right, I should have known she could sense me. I guess I should have known she'd pull a trick on me, too, but I'm so very tired. She tells me she'll be right back. I almost doze off completely before I'm feeling those full supple lips on mine. I pulled her over the couch and into my lap, she could probably feel how much I missed her.

"Christian..." She pouts and I couldn't help but attack her mark. She palms me and that was the final straw as I whisk her upstairs.

The next day, early in the afternoon, she sends me to gather food for tonight and tomorrow. I find the small but stocked grocery store and walk around gathering her list of foods and a few surprises. I still can't get over how small and rural her town is, making my city feel like Los Angeles. I mean being from a small town isn't bad because now hopefully she'll think of my town as a great place to explore plus I have the ocean on my side.

I get back and put everything away. I hear the music upstairs, so I investigate, plus I was hoping to catch her naked.

What can I say? I'm a red-blooded male.

She stands, facing me, stepping closer, possibly about to set the stage for a quick romp, and unwraps her robe, revealing a sexy lingerie set in black.

I'm already so very weak and then she parades around in that? She begs me to make her a snack, pizza bagels to be specific, her big eyes pierce my soul. I nip at her neck as I wrap my arms around her waist. Kas lunges forward but I catch him before he broke the surface but I'm sure she saw my eyes flash.

"Sorry, doll face, I almost lost it. You shouldn't tempt like that." She pouts about the pizza rolls putting her hand on her hip moving and revealing more of her skin. I fall to my knees, kiss, and smack her ass before heading downstairs. She's laughing uncontrollably as she sits back down trying to focus on getting ready.

Thank goddess I had the place furnished. We have a toaster oven and it only took 10-15 minutes before they were piping hot and ready. I put them on a plate and head back upstairs. I was not prepared for what was behind the door. I open it and she turns around from the vanity. "Hello, lover." She says with such a sexy vibration I almost dropped the plate.

Holy fuck she was so sexy in her makeup. She was a bombshell and wasn't even dressed yet. I felt my jealousy creep, I don't want any guys seeing her like this, but she assures me that the look is only for me and that she found the inspiration on Pinterest... whatever that is.

Her robe is still open and I soak in the visual of the lingerie set that will be on the floor later. She pops one in and I immediately take her lips in mine. She looked shocked when I pulled back and gave her my playboy smile.

"What was that for?"

"Do I need a reason? I'm going to get dressed because you're torturing me." I sneak back in later to be under her once more. She pushed me out of the room so she could get dressed.

She knows me well...I'd lock her in and never leave. It would be a 72-hour sex fest. I might still manage at least 24 of those 72.

About 20 minutes later I hear the click of her heels coming down the stairs. I count to five slowly to build up the anticipation before I turn around.

Fuck me and all that is holy. My mouth fell open as I gazed upon a literal angel in my presence. Her curves dominated that short lace dress and only the pure white color kept the dress' innocence. She was one inch away from indecent exposure charges, but she looked so mouth-wateringly sexy.

She's fidgeting nervously, "So, does this look okay?"

That was probably the dumbest question she has asked me. I pull her into my arms and she can probably feel my answer against her, "Oh darlin', you just don't know how fucking sexy you look. Now I really don't want you to go anywhere but I promised you, so let's go." Reluctantly, I pull her towards the door, and we are on our way to Jack's. "Come on, Mrs. Grey, your celebration awaits." I could see the blush forming across her cheeks.

We park and I open her door, she slides down and adjusts her dress which rose significantly, Kas was howling and panting. She takes my hand and we walk towards the bar's saloon doors where a moving wall was standing guard. "Hey, Zeusy!" She hollers at this tree trunk of a security guy.

He could easily snap me in half, at least that's how he's looking at me when he discovers that I'm her husband to be.

"...And you, take care of my girl, she's like a daughter to me and I'll have no problem burying you in a shallow ditch."

Yikes!

Doesn't matter who I am, right now, I'm the guy who better take care of his baby girl. I assure him I will do all I can, whatever to get away from his grasp. She pulls me inside and beelines it toward VIP. Kam and Kayd are there sucking each other's faces.

This will be my first time being around another Legacy, she seems nice, but I wonder if she can sense it. I shake her hand and congratulate her and Kayd on their upcoming wedding.

The girls squeal and do that hug and sway thing, and now...they're crying.

I'm looking for a distraction when Kayd quickly suggests we go get beers. We couldn't move fast enough.

"So," Kayd turns after ordering the beers, "How crazy is it that my girl's best friend is your mate? I did not see that coming. Vanderbilt is a spitfire, but I think you're

the perfect balance for her. Cheers to your engagement."
We clink our bottles.

I watch her saunter over to the other bar where she
seems comfortable with the bartender there. They are
laughing and giggling while he's preparing shots, then
another bartender comes over and I can feel the tension
from here. I will assume that he is an ex because she
flashed her ring and the guy's face fell before he went
back to tending. Kam puts her hand on Nessa's shoulder
and the other bartender waves him off. There's an
interesting story there, I'll have to ask about later.

Nessa screams out something I can't quite make out;
they cheer and knock back a shot. I shake my head while
Kayd and I go back to the VIP section where he
introduces me to his leadership team, Evan, Brent, and
Miles.

"So Christian, is your town as small as ours? Or are you
doing the big city living?" Brent asks me.

"We definitely are not a big city, but we are slightly
larger than here, wouldn't say double but much more and
we have great ocean views."

The music was better tonight, she had influence there.
Before I could focus on the next song, a sexy angel in
her white dress plops down on my lap. She wiggles and I
see it in her eyes, pure lust. She's tempting me while
whispering in my ear, "Can we go now?" She keeps

rubbing against me and it's working more than she knows. Kas is screaming to go home and mate her until the sun rises but I'm holding back for a bit longer.

Contrary to popular belief, I want her to have a blast with her best friend. I want her to laugh, dance, and enjoy being the center of attention. I want her to enjoy herself so much she won't want to immediately return. Her focus will be adapting to the pack and becoming an amazing Luna.

I bounced my knee forcing her to bump against me and she bit her lip to suppress a moan. "Darlin', I promise you after this I am all yours in every possible way your dirty little mind can imagine but this is your time to hang out with your friends before you start your life with me. Go have fun, drink, dance, and then later..."

I lean in and whisper, "You'll be screaming my name until you're hoarse. I'll have to carry you to the jet and even then, we're going to join the mile-high club. You're in for an enormous amount of pleasure." I grinned triumphantly while leaning back and the message was clear on her face. "Fuck me." She whispers and I reply "Later." As I pat her ass to get her off my painful erection.

Sometimes the Moon Goddess likes to take shots at me as punishment because the next thing I know the girls are dancing like strippers against each other but never taking their eyes off us. I look over at Kayd and he is seconds away from snatching Kam and taking her home. He's gripping the side of the chair hard.

"Easy Miller, they're teasing on purpose, but we have the final say. Let's keep them wanting, okay?"

He nods, "You're right. My baby doll always gets her way so she's going to try harder if I don't react like she wants. This will work in my favor later tonight." We share a laugh while toasting our beers as we watch them continue to gyrate against each other.

And we were right, song after song, they continued to take shots and dance against each other as we held conversations while still watching. They eventually stopped to cool down and once again she's in my lap, grinding on me trying to get me to break.

She gives me the sweetest kiss on the cheek, thanking me for allowing her one last night in her hometown.

Two hours later, we prepare to leave. As predicted, the girls are doing the hug swaying thing again but it's more somber this time knowing I was taking her away from her best friend. I promised her full use of the jet any time she wanted to come back and visit.

We barely cross the threshold before I'm seconds from tearing off her clothes. She runs her hands over my abs, and it reminds me of my surprise for her. I step back and undo my shirt revealing a bandage on my chest. She looked alarmed, but I assured her that I'm not injured. I kiss her, deeply and passionately, then take a moment to get lost in her eyes.

"I decided to get this when I was back home, it's something I wanted to have so that if you're not around anyone will know that you're mine and I'm yours. You can take it off." She's skittish about it but I assure her it's not fresh and almost healed. I went to my buddy Johnny's shop; he's done most of my tattoos and so I let him free hand this one.

I had vines surrounding the date we met and below that in script, *'I'll love you forever, my Vanessa, my party girl. You are mine and I am yours, CG'*

It was simple but judging by the tears she loved it. She touches it gently and the sparks course between us.

A couple of days later we're in the car on our way to the airstrip. She's been super quiet and bouncing her leg.

"Chris, I need to tell you something...I've never been on a small jet like yours. I'm...scared."

I immediately squeezed her hand, "Absolutely nothing to fear I promise you. You can meet the pilots and my crew, get the grand tour, and have some herbal tea prepared for you to help you relax. I would never put you in danger, you know that. You are my life." I can see the fear lingering.

When we park, I step out and walk over to her side to open the door. She steps out in her leather pants, cream sweater, and nosebleed heels. I told her the pack was laid back, she said she had to make a great first impression. We walk towards the eight-seater jet. I feel her hands sweat and tremble. I place my hand on her face and she looks up, her eyes tearing up.

"I promise to keep you safe; do you trust me?" She grabs my hand with her ring hand.

I give her a reassuring smile as I kiss her hand. "Absolutely. Just realize I'm not going to let you go during the flight." I chuckle, "You say it as if it's a bad thing. Whatever makes you comfortable on our way home."

I introduced her to the flight crew and my steward. He immediately made some herbal tea and brought her a pillow and a blanket. I insisted we use the bedroom once we were at cruising altitude.

As we taxi her grip tightens, I lift the armrest and bring her close and she closes her eyes to avoid looking out the window. "Did I tell you about the town and all the good stuff there is to do there? I already have a massage session set up for us this weekend and today I'll take you out to see your first California sunset, it will take your breath away. You cannot compare its beauty. You'll be..." I look down and she fell asleep which was great because we had hit turbulence. I carry her back to the bedroom and pull her shoes off. It was a small room with a tv and a bed, the bathroom right outside the door. I lay her down and pull off my shirt, she wriggles around and whimpers. "Christian..." My touch comforts her as she drifts comfortably back to sleep.

Sometime later I shift to face her and she's wide awake. She kisses my nose, "Thank you."

I stretch, then pull her to me, "For what?"

"For making me so comfortable that I fell asleep. The sound of your heartbeat and your scent were the perfect combination. How much longer?"

Just then there was a knock, "Alpha Grey we are 20 minutes from landing."

I smile, "There's your answer, come on." She stands up, stretches, and I got a peek of her smooth skin up to the bottom of her blue lace bra.

We landed and arrived next to one of my awaiting cars, which means one of or all my guys are here. I should have known. Please don't let them embarrass me. I sigh long and hard as she's putting on her heels. "What's wrong?"

"Nothing...my leadership might be out there. They're up to no good, I know it. Ready to spill the beans." She bursts out laughing, "Oh honey, relax...they're going to tell all your embarrassing stories eventually, deal with it. Come on, let's go home."

I pull her close, "Say it again."

"What? Let's go home."

I kiss her fervently then pat her ass. "Come on, let's go."

As we walked out, I saw all three of them, I knew it. I'm going to kill them. I plaster on a fake smile.

"Gentlemen, this is Vanessa, my Nessa, and your Luna."

Fitz shakes her hand then bows like a mid-century knight, "Greetings Luna Nessa, welcome home. It is an honor to be in your presence."

I smack his hand, "Kiss ass."

"Stop it, they're being polite." She smiles and kisses me quickly, "Let's go, gentleman." I look over to three grinning idiots.

Nes and I ride in the back seat with Fitz and the twins up front. I couldn't help but snuggle up against her, causing her to squeal. "Chris...stop..."

"Oh, brother!" Fitz pretends he's dry heaving. She taps my chest, "Alright, enough couple stuff. So, guys tell me, where do you hang out on a Friday night?"

"Oh, we usually go to our strip bar, Leather & Lace."

Shit!

I look over ready to face the why I didn't tell her I owned a strip club, but she merely nods. "Cool, I'd like to go sometime. Do they have an amateur night?"

Everyone gasped except me. "Not a chance in Hell, darlin', unmated dancers only. I will put a pole in our bedroom if you desire to dance so badly. I hear I tip very nicely."

She rolls her eyes. "Fine, I want one in our room."

Eventually, we pull up to the house and the pack is outside and waiting. I can't tell if it is the entire pack but it's a good majority.

"Wow, that's a lot of strangers." She grimaces and I run my fingers through the hair that frames her face. "Don't worry, they'll love you as much as I do."

"Yeah, except for the girls who thought they were next in line!" Kirin laughs and Kellan follows until they look back at me. I am not amused. That was not funny in the least bit. That's all I need is to plant the seed of self-doubt.

"Sorry, it was a bad joke." He shrinks back in his seat and Kellan looks out the window to avoid my glare.

She breaks up the tension by laughing, "Don't worry I'm sure he's had his fun...I did, but that's the past. Well, I can't avoid the inevitable...let's do this."

I open the door and step out. Holding out my hand for her to grab. She scoots over the seat then steps out with the most radiant smile and the twins pull the truck away as we stand in front of the pack.

"Good afternoon members of the Midnight Shadow Pack. Please welcome your Luna, Vanessa Vanderbilt. Show her the same respect you would for your Alpha."

They all bow in unison. "Greetings and welcome to the Midnight Shadow Pack Luna Vanessa." I feel immense pride in my pack. I verbalize my appreciation and dismiss them.

"Come on, let's get you situated before the sun sets." She follows me into the house, the sound of her heels does something to me as we head to the elevator. I usually never use it, but I didn't want her to take the steps in those shoes.

Once in front of the bedroom doors, she giggles, "It's like the vacation house all over again. Except these doors are huge and solid." I stand close behind her and she opens it up to the masterpiece that Cameron designed for us.

"Wow, it's absolutely beautiful in here! You said your pack sister did this? Where is she?" She walks around as if in a museum. I call Cameron to the room. She happily skips around the corner, "Hey big bro, you called me?" I point ahead as Nessa comes from the bathroom.

"You must be Cameron! Let me tell you, this place is beautiful, and I love everything about it! I hope you realize how talented you are. This could be an amazing career for you!"

Cameron bows, "Why thank you, Luna Vanessa! I'm so glad you are pleased with my work because *someone* was very hesitant to get out of my way to do my job."

Now they're both staring at me.

"Whoa, wait a minute! It was super early that morning! She kicked me out of my own room!" I grumble as they laugh together, I'm being double-teamed already.

Nessa takes my hand, "Oh sweetheart, it's okay. Thank you, Cameron, for all your hard work. I'm going to change out of my travel clothes."

As she walks into the bathroom I turn and Cameron's already out the door before I can chastise her. I hear the shower and suddenly my pulse is racing. Should we christen the shower? She knows by now I'm damn sure going to try!

Later, she's in a white linen sundress and brown gladiator sandals, leaving her beautiful curls half up/half down.

I found some cargo pants and a white button-down, outside of my usual. I keep other clothing, I prefer to wear black, but this was a special occasion.

"Ooh, look at my Alpha, it's still weird to see you not wearing black, but you do look handsome." She bows like the pack did but the way she did it was flirtatious and seductive. She's asking for a night in, I can always order room service.

"I figured I'd try to match the stunning beauty of my fiancée. Come on, it's near twilight." We walk outside and turn right toward the cliff. The wind whips her hair and dress around.

"Oh, my goddess. I could listen to this forever." She gasps once we're near the edge and she's in awe of the view. The deep blue waves crash against the cliff, creating a white foam, the boats on the horizon making their way to the ports, and the seagulls soaring and then diving into the ocean to get their next meal.

I wrap her up in my arms and sway as we watch the landscape change from bold yellows and oranges to deep reds and purples as it fades under the horizon. "It's beautiful."

I squeeze her hip to get her attention away from the view, whispering gently, "I am yours and you are mine, forever and a day. I love you, darlin'." At the perfect moment, I dip and kiss her passionately. She holds on tight until the last ray is gone, and the sky opens up to the stars. I set her back on her feet and she's breathing as hard as me. "Wow, that was some kiss. Best end of the day moment ever."

I couldn't help but smile, her first memorable moment in our home.

"Chris, before we eat, there's someone I want you to meet…"

"What do you mean? Are you pregnant? I thought I would be able to sense that..." I sniffed around her to see if I could pick up anything.

She laughs, "No. I mean, I'm a hybrid, half-werewolf and…"

She steps back and closes her eyes; her hair falls bone straight and turns silver. And now her eyes matched her icy locks when she revealed them again as a breeze from nowhere whipped her hair around dramatically.

"Greetings Alpha, I am Calliope, her silver moon witch. I am her warrior, her protector."

Not knowing what to say I nod. She reverts back, "Now you know, I didn't want to keep something that important from you. I know some people frown at hybrids and now that I'm a part of your pack, I didn't want any of your members…" I cut her off with a kiss, "You're safe here. You being a hybrid only makes us stronger, now let's eat."

I let her walk ahead of me, I felt excruciatingly guilty for not telling her of my own status, but I couldn't relay that tidbit of information yet, especially when I was having trouble with my own sorcerer. And I need to figure out why I have this deep dark feeling in the pit of my stomach.

I had to be careful because although she was a witch, her witch may sense my Legacy. That could cause a major uproar especially the 'keeping it a secret from her' part.

Dinner that night was buffet style, it was a way for her to introduce herself to people. She would talk while they fixed their plates.

When we finally walked into the dining hall. She held her hand up to stop them from standing, "Please, sit and eat! I'm not as formal as our Alpha here." She smiles at me as she kisses my cheek. "Very funny. They are figuring out how to act around you."

"Oh, we can nip that in the bud right now." She taps her glass gaining everyone's attention. "First, thank you for that warm greeting earlier, I was a bit apprehensive, but I appreciate your kindness and respect. I know I've only been around a few hours, but I am absolutely in love with our Alpha and his pack is my pack. I am here to learn but also to nurture. If you feel comfortable, please call me Luna Nessa or simply Nessa. Respect is earned and given. I want you to be comfortable coming to me because I will be coming to some of you with questions to get the lay of the land. I am proud to be a new member of this great pack, thank you so much." She places her hand on her heart and bows before sitting back down.

I rarely do PDA, but I kiss her gently, "That was well said, darlin'. We are proud to have you by my side." The rest of the dinner went smoothly, she even went into the living room to watch a movie with some pack members. I had some work to finish so I went to hole up in my office.

Around 10 p.m., I'm still knee-deep in proposals, propositions, and signing approved memos when I hear my door creak open, no-knock, which irritates me to no end, but then I hear the distinct sound of heels. My nostrils flare as her scent hits me along with the jasmine perfume she always wears.

She's in skintight black leather capris, a black corset that stops at her belly button, a cropped fitted white leather jacket, and of course, her nosebleed black heels.

I was so turned on I couldn't even say anything. My body shuddered at the sight of her. I am looking into the eyes of my pure unadulterated vixen.

The twins and Fitz trail behind her. They better keep their eyes to themselves because that view is all mine.

"For fucks sake, darlin'."

She saunters over and leans over my desk, kicking her heel up with her breasts pressed together by her outstretched arms holding her up. She knew what she was doing.

"We're going out, I want to see if your favorite place is better than Jack's and I want to see my competition." A smirk forms across her face before she ran her tongue across her ruby red lips.

I put my pen down and lean back in my chair, putting my hands behind my head. "I told you I never dated any dancer. Demi is the only dancer I am close to and that's because her husband died protecting the pack, she's family."

She smiles in delight, "That's even better, they can set eyes on the hottest bitch in town. Come on or we leave without you." She stands up straight fixing her outfit.

I stood up so quickly not caring if she saw her effect on me, "You leave with her, I'll toss you over the cliff. Besides, your sexy ass is riding with me. The twins can take... the Ferrari."

They high-fived quickly and rushed downstairs to get the keys to my cherry red SF90 Stradale. It can go 0-100 in 2.5 seconds, it's an adrenaline rush and for them, a chick magnet. My guys, always trying to get laid. What can I say? I have a set of strong red-blooded males in my leadership. It'll be interesting when they're all caught up like me.

As the door closes, I think she realizes it's only the two of us and she's in trouble with no one to save her. I growl, low and long, fair warning she has tempted her beast and my beauty was about to be whisked away to the confines of our bedroom.

Before she could get away I had her in my arms, my hands sliding across the smooth skin showing and squeezing her ass in those pants that were practically a second skin. Then I realized…there were NO panty lines. She winks when my eyes meet hers.

She pulls me out of the office and right into the bathroom but didn't follow. She gives me a knowing look, it's an unspoken agreement for later. Twenty minutes later I am ready. Fitz is already on his bike and ready to go while I pull my baby out the garage. My eyes follow as Nessa strolls over to my bike. I'm talking to Fitz as she lays on her back, arching it. Her hand reaches back towards the handlebars. She kicks up one heel on the seat. It's a scene from a wet dream I tell you and then she purrs, "Hot, right? Straight out of one of those magazines right before you turn the page and she's completely naked. I've always wanted to pose on a bike like this."

My mind wanders to how I could get that X-rated shot on my bike. I took a few pics at her request and for my benefit. She sits up so I can put on her helmet and then I slide in front of her. "Hold on tight, darlin'."

We lead the way out the gates and down into town. She's wrapped around me tight and I can hear her squealing in excitement. I take a straightaway at 80 mph until I feel her grip get tighter, so I back off again. Once we get to Leather & Lace, she flips her head forward and fluffs her curls back up. Everything she does seems so blatantly sexy, but I think she does that to show off. She teases me as she pulls down the corset, showcasing her amazing rack.

"Hey! Eyes up here, mister!"

I grab and kiss her softly. I feel her melt into me, "Not a chance, especially when you got them out for everyone to see. You might cause a brawl tonight if they look at you wrong."

"Chris...I want to have fun. I promise this is all for you and only you...but I also want them to see what a fox the Alpha has for a mate." She slips out of my grip and walks away towards where the guys were standing. I shake out my locs and follow behind her.

The bouncer unclips the velvet rope, "Alpha, your table is ready."

I pointed to her, "Thanks, this is my mate, Vanessa."

He smiles and bows, "Welcome Luna Vanessa, so pleased to meet you, I've only heard good things." She grabs his hand and shakes it, a growl escapes. Kas agrees, no one touches our mate.

She rolls her eyes at me, "Ignore him, it was nice to meet you." She walks in and starts dancing. I could tell this would be torture because all eyes were on her and a few look like they were contemplating approaching the banging new girl until I walked in and relayed through link she was off-limits unless they wanted to die a slow, acid-dripping death or me ripping their heart out.

Suddenly she spins on her heels to glare at me, I forgot to block her link. *Shit!* She beckons for me to come here; I feel like a scolded puppy. "You're about to lose your after-hour privileges, stop being such a...caveman. I would never look at anyone else and no one would dare disrespect their Alpha. Okay?" I know she's right but sometimes the possessive caveman genes win. Her kiss melts me before I guide her to the table center to the stage. Her brow raises when I signal the DJ to cancel first dibs.

I shrug my shoulders, "It's a long story and a perk of being a, once single, Alpha." She leans into me and is so close I can taste the essence of her lip gloss, it's strawberry scented. "Uh-huh..." She leans back when the waitress approaches to take our drink order. I order a double shot of Highland Park dark whiskey and she orders a dirty little slut; I don't even know what that is, but it sounds sinful. Like her.

The current dancer finishes and the DJ announces Eve to the stage. "This is Demi, the one I was telling you about."

Demi steps onto the stage with great applause which intrigues Nessa. She sits forward like a student being taught the sensual art of erotic teasing. She was mentally taking notes, especially because I promised that pole in our room.

Demi goes into her rock routine as the music transitions. She has a dance for several genres of music, but rock was her most popular. A good indication were the littered bills covering the floor. With *American Woman* blasting, she went from her floor to her pole routine.

"There's no way this badass is in her forties!" She watches her spin around the pole and drop into a split. The men went wild, whistling, hooting, and hollering. "Oh, she's definitely going to be my pole instructor! And in five-inch heels too, yes!" She whistles out loud, it's louder than anyone else which grabs Demi's attention. She sends us a friendly smile.

"Gimme money!" Nessa yells while holding out her hand waiting for me. I pulled out two, hundred-dollar bills. She saunters over and Eve slides seductively off the pole and crawls toward Nes.

Demi stops in front of Nes, turns, and lies on her back with her head hanging off the stage. It was getting interesting...

Nes takes a bill and slips it into Demi's tiny star-spangled bikini top and Demi teasingly jiggles her breasts together. Their lewd behavior grabs everyone's attention. Kirin drops his beer at the bar, but the bartender replaces it.

Demi slides up to her knees as Nessa puts the other bill between her own delectable breasts and Demi leans ever closer, motorboating them before grabbing the bill with her teeth. Nessa squeals then high fives her.

What in the porn fantasy is going on here?!

It was hot and I had a raging boner like a freaking teenager.

And this night is over.

I radio that I'm leaving but they already knew that. Demi and Nes are laughing and chatting after her set by the bar. I hope Demi isn't telling embarrassing stories about me. Doesn't matter, I am on a mission. I wrap my arm around Nes. "Hey Demi, great set. Bye, Demi." She smiles knowingly but Nessa doesn't. "Talk to you later. Nice meeting you, Luna. Enjoy the rest of your night."

Nessa is still in the dark, "But we just got here." She stated as I pulled her out the door, I refused to look back because I know her breasts are bouncing heavily just shy of popping out and I promise I'll get a room at the bed & breakfast nearby, but I look forward to christening our bedroom. I finally pin her against my bike, taking a moment to soak in all her sexiness. She bit her lip; I think she was finally getting my message.

I see the glow of my eyes in the reflection from how wide her pupils were, Kas has taken over. I'll need to gain control before we get home. Just when I think we've got her cornered, Nes palms me, "Ooh, you ready to go home and break in our new bed?" Her eyes flash, Dalila was close to the surface.

I attack her neck and feel a slight buckle in her knees before she slides into position on my bike. She's panting before we hit pack grounds. The hum of the engine between her legs keeps her worked up and I rev it often. I can hear her purring moans over the engine. Her hand is squeezing my inner thigh and she's basically stroking me because I've been hard the entire time... I am on a hair-trigger.

When we get home, she slides off seductively, hands me the helmet, and walks towards the front door. I'm almost lost in the rhythmic sway of her hips, but I force myself to push my bike back into the garage. All the while she's torturing me by linking me her explicit thoughts.

I walk in to see her sexy stilettos next to the door. As I head towards the staircase, I notice something hanging off the stair post, it was her badass leather jacket. I grab it and climb the stairs two at a time then I see something else laying near the door, it's her corset. The luckiest piece of fabric squeezing her into that seductive hourglass figure. Solidifying I was blessed with the woman that fit me best. A siren, a seductress, a pit bull in heels when she needed to be but most important, she was mine.

I get a whiff of her scent and groan as I open the door. The entire room was dark except for the moon peeking through the sheer curtains of the balcony. The ceiling fan molded the sheets to her body. I couldn't tell if she was pretending to sleep or fell asleep. Either way, I'll play her game.

I toss her clothes in the chair then I strip out of everything. I slip under the sheets and kiss her from her feet, caressing her smooth skin upward. She stirs with her cute little giggles and moans. "Mmm, I almost fell asleep..."

"Not after your little performance at the club. I'm nowhere near done with you...so..." I flip her and now her eyes are wide open as she anticipates my touch where she wants me. She squirms. I give her that bad boy smirk that drives her wild and she rolls her eyes trying to pretend it doesn't affect her. It drives her crazy.

"Tell me what you want, Nes." Her breath hitches as I tease, waiting for her answer. I work her up to the very brink, making it impossible to respond so I pull back and she pouts. "Chrissss, I was so close."

"I asked you a question, darlin'. I want to hear what you want from me."

She sits up on her elbows, gazing at me, licking her lips. Her body is amazing and it's hard for me not to dive in and fulfill my every fantasy. The silk sheets slipped down to pool at her abdomen, leaving her breasts on display and I forced myself to maintain eye contact.

She laughs at my reaction, "Fine, I'll tell you exactly what I want. I want my mate to claim what is his in the space we now call ours. In our pack house, in our room, in our bed. I want your name to become a mantra I can't stop moaning over and over until I'm completely breathless. Please...don't make me wait any longer."

Her response made me want her even more if that's possible. My mate needs me as much as I need her, she adores me as much as I, her. Now I will spend these early hours showing her how much.

Twelve months later:

A year flies by when your life seems complete. The only stressors seem around the time of annual physicals, but I left that task to Fitz this year. He and the twins have taken over most of the non-Alpha-related responsibilities which leaves me more time to focus on pressing issues. Most important, I can concentrate on my Luna and our lives together.

I wanted to make sure she knew how much she meant and how having her here has only made our pack stronger. I felt like because I didn't see it from my parents I had to go above and beyond. I won't say my father didn't love my mother, as cold and emotionless as he was with me, there were flashes of love and adoration for her. I'd like to think he would at least show it behind closed doors. I would never be like him.

Anyway, Nes has grown substantially in learning her duties and the way the pack runs. She has made friends with many females of the pack. Well, the ones who weren't pissed about her squashing their fantasies of waking up in my bed. She had grown tired of the whispers and side eyes, so she broadcast over the pack link that if anyone had something to say or wanted to fight for a chance at me it was now or never. She told me if anyone was bold enough, she'd 'rip that bitch to shreds and then incinerate her.' She said it with a big smile on her face and a glint of violence in her eyes. I thought maybe Calliope had slipped past, but her hair had not turned indicating she was in charge. No, that was my little hellcat.

No one was that bold or stupid to meet her outside near the training area. Those who were unhappy would have to tuck their tails between their legs and keep their mouths shut.

Or at least that would be my suggestion.

During the day she loves to stop by the nursery and check in on the pack pups. I can hear her thoughts and excitement when she's with them. They love seeing "Miss Nessa". I took a break one day and watched from the window hoping my scent wouldn't give me away. I watched her eyes light up when they corral around her. She knelt to give each a forehead kiss and then took them to the reading corner and read them a book about a caterpillar. She was made for motherhood.

I know what she's thinking but she won't bring it up. Part of me believes she's scared but when she video chats Kam I see her enthusiasm over everything, the good and the bad. When she interacts with Kam's twins they always giggle and laugh, they naturally love her and she loves seeing their newest milestone, which this time was waving when she waved at them. I know she will make an amazing mother.

We'll have that discussion another time because tonight is super special, it is one of our one-year anniversaries. It was one year ago she was welcomed on pack ground. I had the chef prepare a special meal and set up a table near the cliff side for a moonlit dinner.

I'm sitting on our bed waiting for her, "Nes, we're going to be late for our own anniversary dinner."

"I'm coming, give me a minute! Why don't you go downstairs!" She sounds annoyed.

I shrug my shoulders as I near the bathroom door, I give it a tap, "You sure you're okay?"

"I said I'm fine...just... meet me downstairs!"

O...kay, not going to shake that hornet's nest.

I'm on my phone when the elevator door dings and she steps out.

That is the littlest black dress I've ever seen, it's sheer, it's lace, it's downright illegal.

"Well...hello gorgeous. You look stunning, my darlin'." I spin her to get the full view.

"Okay, enough spinning, you're making me queasy. Lead the way."

I hold her hand as we walk out to our romantic setting. I had a pathway installed to the table near the cliff so it would be easier for her to navigate in her heels. Once seated the staff brings our entrees and light the candles on the table. Luckily the wind had died down to a gentle breeze.

I open my hand and she places her hand in mine, the electric current of our bond is intense. We eat dinner like that and at the end of dessert, I pull my hand away to retrieve her gift.

"My Nessa, no gift could explain how special you are to me, but I hope this is a good start." I slide over the oblong blue velvet box, and she glances at me before opening it, revealing the half carat diamond solitaire infinity pendant necklace. It is attached to a sterling silver chain. It's beautifully delicate as I stand behind to place it around her neck. She moves her fiery hair over as she watches me from her phone camera, taking a picture of the moment she admired her gift from me. "Happy anniversary, my love." She's sniffling, wiping away the tears. "Thank you, sweetheart, it's so beautiful. Now sit down, I need your full attention for my gift to you."

I do as she says when she slides over a box almost similar in size to the one I gave her, except it was wrapped in black paper. I assume it's a nice watch, she knows I have a thing for watches, especially vintage, small-batch ones. The rarer the better. Then she perches herself on my lap, her scandalously short dress even shorter. My hand is now on her upper thigh and I feel no trace of her dress. Thank Goddess we're alone.

I look up as she grazes my collarbone, "This is something that marks the beginning of a new chapter for us. Happy anniversary, Christian." I was trying to figure out how a watch could do that, but I gave up and opened the nicely wrapped box that held the answer. It made the red bow I slapped on my gift look sloppy and thrown together. I tilt my head when I open the gift. It's...a white stick? With...two solid pink lines. I'm no rocket scientist but…

No way.

I look at the test, then her, then the test again.

"Really?!"

She places my hand on her stomach.

"Yes, really." Her eyes well with tears.

SHE'S PREGNANT!

I pull her into me, kissing her incessantly as we celebrate that, "I'm going to be a daddy! How far along are you? When did this happen?"

I was almost hyperventilating in my joy, I felt it all, the entire range of emotion.

Now she's giggling hard, holding her stomach. "First, let's breathe, I don't need you passing out. I'm barely four weeks...remember the night you wanted to play the pizza delivery guy? Yeah...you delivered more than the pizza."

I pick her up and spin her. "This is the best news ever!"

She taps my chest as a signal to put her down. "Enough spinning, I told you it makes me queasy and now you know why." She clutches her stomach and I rub it hoping the nausea subsides.

I linked my boys and told them immediately and they offered us their congratulations. If I could, I'd scream it from the mountain top, but a cliff will do.

I puff out my chest and feel the need to announce that I've marked my territory, "I'm going to be a father!"

It sounds good, it feels even better. She calls me back a little concerned at how close I am to the edge. That night I wrap myself up in the woman carrying our future, an actual Legacy.

The guilt hits me hard when I realize that I am now forced to tell her the truth. She's going to have a much shorter pregnancy and it explains why I couldn't sense it as the Legacy protects itself by masking themselves.

I want to ensure they are not in danger. Things have been radio silent for quite a while. Damien has kept to himself and Tavi seems to be keeping the peace with Kas. Maybe I was overreacting or stressing over nonsense.

Besides learning about pregnancy and motherhood, Nessa needed to finish learning her official responsibilities as my Luna. Since my mother was no longer with us, Nessa could only get her certified Luna teachings from our elder, Miss Ren. She taught my mother and a few Lunas from other packs in the region. That gave Nessa enough time to acclimate and learn what she could from the females of the pack until Miss Ren's schedule was free. Miss Ren and a few other ladies were blessed with teaching the ins and outs of being a Luna without being designated as one. It was a divine gift.

Miss Ren is the epitome of a sweet old lady, she doesn't look powerful, but she is filled with decades of knowledge and practice, she's probably stronger than me at full Legacy. She reminded us to meet her in the morning. I could see the worry on Nes' face, but I assured her it would be fine.

"Good morning, Alpha. Luna Vanessa. I assure you that you have nothing to worry about, dear." Nessa gasped but Miss Ren tapped her temple and smiled. Of course, she knew. "Now that you have become comfortable in your surroundings, I will be teaching you all it is to be a superb Luna. But first…" She closed her eyes and smiled before opening them again, "You're a hybrid, silver witch and wolf, a most powerful combination. You will be a great ally to our pack. Come, we will start with the basics. Alpha Grey, come back at 7 p.m."

I agree as they chat while walking away. I could tell Nessa was intrigued at how she could sense all that and perhaps how she could learn. She was in for a long day but that gives me time to finally do some work. I need to buckle down and focus. I can get those pack proposals out and review the specs on a property in town that could be a great investment.

I got a ton of taskings done before my eyes were burning from working too hard and fast. I was proud of the work I got done. I even had time to hit the gym with the guys. We usually amp up our workouts before the summer to flex our progress at the pool. It would be a little different for me but not an excuse to slack off.

I decided, with one hour left, to go downstairs and cook us a personal dinner. I sauteed shrimp with a mushroom and garlic marinara sauce to go over linguine and topped with fresh parmesan. I went to the cellar to find a good pinot for me and a non-alcoholic sangria mocktail for the mom to be. Once everything was done, I sent the food and drinks up to our room and I waited against the kitchen island as they approached.

They both have huge smiles on their faces. "Alpha, she's going to be an amazing Luna! I predict maybe two weeks of lessons. Probably not even that and luckily, I freed up my schedule, no other Lunas are scheduled until next month. Luna Nessa, we will meet again the day after tomorrow. Rest up, you had a long day today, they won't all be that lengthy. Have a wonderful night you two." She pats my cheek before taking her leave. Her gentle voice and beautiful smile remind me so much of my Nana, but I can't think about her...it hurts too much.

Nessa squeezes my hand and sighs. "Wow, I've got so much to learn! But Miss Ren assured me with guidance I could be amazing. Who knew?! So, are you hungry? I can whip up something really quick."

I chuckle as I pull her toward me and kiss her gently. She looks confused. "I already cooked for us. It's upstairs." Her eyes showed shock, "You cooked? For me?" I surprised her further by picking her up bridal style and carrying her to our room.

Around 3 a.m., I'm awakened by the one sound I dread, especially now that she is here, the intrusion alarm. I shoot up and roar, linking for an immediate update. I turn to her side to see if my outburst startled her. I get a reply from Fitz telling me I need to come quick. I panic stating that Nes is missing but he assures me she isn't. I raced out to the tree line, "Fitz!"

"Over here, boss!"

I approach to see Fitz, the twins, and one of the security teams. They are surrounding something that's...burning? I see the wispy smoke, but I also see the horrific expressions on their pale faces. Fitz has them part so I can see why.

For the love of Moon Goddess...

Lying on the ground are two bodies burned beyond recognition except for pieces of bone and their skulls. I have never seen someone mutilated like that before and I've tortured plenty of my enemies. This was impressive in a sick and twisted way.

"What the hell happened? Who did this?" Fitz points to his left and there's Nessa in her sleeping gown, casually leaning against the tree filing her nails still in her witch. Her hair was blowing in the wind but there was no breeze. Quite the dramatic reveal for those unaware of her hybrid status which was everyone in the immediate area.

"You're welcome. I heard them a mile away. I wanted to see how much information I could get from them before I punished them."

I approached slowly, knowing we hadn't established our relationship, I needed to be cautious.

"No need to pussy foot around me, Alpha. I know how important you are to my host. I will get her for you." Her hair changes back and I'm staring into familiar eyes again. I ignore the audible gasps and stares. "Darlin', you were supposed to be in bed."

"I was until Dalila sensed some movement outside and Calliope wanted answers. So, we popped up over there and waited for them." She points at the break in the trees.

"And then?" I dismissed everyone and had them call the cleanup crew for immediate disposal. I'd have to pay them extra for this and probably a week's vacation. I'd need a break if I saw this.

She snaps her fingers, bringing me out of my thoughts. "They were looking for your hall of records and so I stepped out warning them that they should leave and there wouldn't be a problem. The giant idiot said, 'You would make a fine concubine. Somebody better come claim their pretty little birdie before someone else does'. I told him that threatening the Luna of this pack was a big mistake and he said 'There is no Luna to this pack! You're probably some whore who's sleeping with him, he has plenty of she-wolves to satisfy his needs. You're just another number."

She eyes me, and I realize it's not her who raises her brow as they flash silver momentarily. Calliope was not happy about that tidbit of information. I feel this will turn into a conversation later. To be fair, I wasn't some man whore, but I had my fun. Rumors are all they are.

"Anyway, I laugh and say that news doesn't travel fast wherever they are from and that I am indeed the Luna of this pack and not some trashy whore. I warned them that they made a very fatal mistake in underestimating me and then...I set them on fire from the inside out." She said it with so much enthusiasm and that sinister smile that reminds me a bit of my father except she was being protective not destructive. She waves her hand as she continues, "I've been wanting to use that spell, too. It's brutal but it sends the message. Disrespect my Alpha or me and I'll end you. Let's go, it's starting to smell. I don't want it in my hair and it's making the baby nauseous." She seemed nonchalant as she walked past the charred remains. It was then I realized how powerful she was.

I pull her back and surprise her with a kiss, my mind is spinning. "Goddess, I love you so much. Let's get married next week." She laughs, almost doubled over in hysterics, and then stops when she sees I'm not laughing. "Oh, you're serious? Chris, you know my Luna ceremony is next week." I frown feeling disappointed, but I knew how important that was, to recognize her completion of her training and her official crowning. I nod my head, but she squeezes my hand, giving me a small smile. "How about the week after? I'll be more than happy to officially be yours in two weeks. I need to see if I can get Kayd to clear Kam to fly. I need my maid of honor; besides, I don't even have my dress picked out. Deal?"

"Absolutely, besides after seeing what you can do, I'm not about to get on Calliope's bad side."

She pulls me, "Come on, let's go, I'm sure they need a statement before I go back to bed. Mommy is tired." Her first reference to her newest title and it sounds so sweet.

"You're right. You do that and I'm going to set up a little trip to see 'Alpha' Damien and end this once and for all. If he wants a war, he'll get it!"

I summon my leadership to meet me in my office. Fitz is pacing trying to find the words but then blurts out, "Dude, what the fuck?! You didn't say she was a hybrid! She's scarier than you, did you see how she fricasseed them!"

"Yeah! Was that her witch?! Will she be a liability? Because she doesn't seem reigned in." Kirin agrees to what Kellan says.

"I assure you Calliope is her protector and wants nothing but the safety of our pack. I haven't known for long, she revealed herself then asked if there were any other hybrids and...I said there weren't." I could see it, but I held my hand up. "I know, I know. I will reveal everything soon. The wedding is in two weeks but first a more pressing matter. I'm going to Damien's and set him straight once and for all. Whatever his end game is, I'm not interested, unless it's tearing him apart."

We're interrupted by a gentle knock on the door, "Sweetheart?" She pauses and closes her robe tighter when she sees the guys. "Hey, sorry, you guys are having a meeting. I'm going to bed; I'll see you soon?" I do my best to wrap things up here quickly. The twins are cheesing hard and I dismiss everyone, we could all use a good night's sleep after this.

Flash forward two weeks, the week prior we held her Luna ceremony. She looked impeccable in her fit and flare ice blue dress. She made her way to the stage and pledged her allegiance to the pack and her King. I was honored to crown her as my Queen and formally introduce her to the entire pack.

Now I'm waiting at the altar now for my bride to be. We held our ceremony in the garden where nature culminated in the beautiful tulips, roses, and hydrangeas. The bright pops of color against the all-white staging. Except me, of course. You guessed it, a classic black satin peak lapel suit and no tie.

I watch Kam make her way to the altar in a sleek simple magenta bridesmaid dress. Kayd watches in awe as she passes him and gives him a mischievous smile. This is mommy and daddy's first outing since the twins, they deserve to have a little adult fun. Kam turns to my right and takes her place.

Next are the ring boy and flower girl, they are the kids of my pack members. Then a deafening silence before the chime of the bells to signal her arrival. Because we are outside, I watch her come around the corner of the trellis adorned in hibiscus and snapdragons.

I have never laid eyes on something more breathtaking in my life. As soon as our eyes meet, I feel the lump in my throat. I can see the tears slide down her cheeks as she walks towards me. The happiness that radiated from her consumed me as she came closer. I meet her at the bottom of the stairs, she takes my hand, and we face the reverend to begin the ceremony.

"I now pronounce you husband and wife. Alpha, you may kiss your bride as we welcome Mr. and Mrs. Christian Evan Grey." I kept our kiss innocent because there were children around, I'd have her later.

Kam straightens out Nessa's dress as she turns so we can walk back down the aisle. Kayd stands and hooks his arm around Kam and they follow us to the reception area.

I made a quick detour and let her walk ahead of me into the honeymoon suite. All weddings here give the couple the option to use the suite as a pre-honeymoon getaway. It has all the amenities of an Executive King Suite.

She squeals, "It's official! I'm all yours!" She bounces up and down and my eyes are glued to her...well, when I look up, she knows.

"Really, Mr. Grey. Not even five seconds after making it official?"

I sidled up to her, wrapping her in my arms. "Come on, Mrs. Grey, I simply wanted some alone time with my wife before we're stuck saying a million thank you's before I can...mark my territory."

"Haven't you done enough! You'll have your way later, the sooner we go out there, the sooner we can get back."

She has a point. "Ugh...fine..." I plaster on a cheesy smile as she pulls me out to the reception hall.

A few days later, I convinced Nessa to stay home while I took care of 'Alpha' Damien. She wanted to come with me, but this is a side of me I don't want her to see. I will try to keep my cool and stay diplomatic. Keyword is try.

Fitz accompanied me to Lovenshire, I told Miller what my intentions were and that I didn't want to involve him unnecessarily especially with him being local. He agreed but offered his services if an emergency arose.

I neglected to notify Damien of my visit, on purpose, to further express my disdain for his actions and the sincerity of my threat. He may have animosity towards me because of Bambi but he should have known that his plan with her had deadly consequences.

We approach his mediocre home, there's no gate, gate guards, no form of protection, not even a fence.

Pathetic.

I knock loudly and wait. Then, nothing. Tired of waiting, Fitz bangs on the door hard.

"What the hell?" Damien screams. Fitz shrugs as I watch a figure approach the door finally.

The door opens and behold I am in the presence of... "Damien," I state flatly.

He sneers as his lip curls, "That's *Alpha* Damien, Alpha Grey. I suggest you respect me as I would you, seeing that you are currently at MY door on MY land."

I scoff, if he wants respect, he'll never get it. The title of Alpha is prestigious, passed down to the next, you don't "make" yourself an Alpha. He's nothing more than a laughingstock. Truth be told he probably stole this house and property, too. I try to stick to my goal of being diplomatic, but he's already tap dancing on the landmine.

"May we come in and discuss your egregious actions towards my pack with subsequent reactions?"

He steps away from the door and we follow him down the tiny corridor into his office. The place looks like a standard farmhouse but covered in a year's worth of dust. He could at least have one of his lackeys keep the place clean, but I digress.

"Have a seat. I take it you're here to discuss the whereabouts of my niece."

I sit down on the sofa with Fitz beside me as Damien sits across from us in the chair behind his desk. It's a dark rich finished solid oak with antique varnish, he splurged to have his office resemble that of the rest of the Alphas. Except in ¼ of the space.

"Let's not waste my time. You know exactly what happened to your precious niece. Why would you send her after the 'disappearance' of the others? They never come back…and neither will she, not whole, anyway." I taper off to let that revelation sink in. "So, what is it that you want from me?" I knew what he wanted. I needed final confirmation.

Damien leans forward, like he was about to disclose top secret government information. "I have a plan to overthrow Miller and his elitist Cheshire Pack. I think we can take them down especially with your powers and all." He was trying to coax me, but I would not budge. Fitz links me laughing at how stupid Damien thinks I am.

"And then what? Say this crackpot plan of yours worked, what next? I'll answer that, you'd stab me in the back so that you can take that #1 position. I'm not stupid, *Alpha*. Besides, you have no power, all you have are minions and kiss asses, a shack of a house, and a sad attempt to show your face pretending to be relevant. You don't have the resources nor the gall to overthrow Kayden Miller on your own. And you think I would sacrifice my pack to have you eventually turn on me and look like a fool? Let me make this absolutely clear, which I thought I had when I sent my message back to you in the blood of your niece!" Damian shot up baring his teeth but did not move from behind his desk. All bark and no bite. I keep calm because even my golden eyes could be mistaken for amber and would give him more ammunition to move forward.

I step forward and stand in front of his desk, tapping it to make my point. "In no way, shape, or form will I assist you in your hair-brained plan, I suggest you cease and desist with whatever you are looking for in my compound, you will not be happy with what you find. The next time will be your first move in a war and I will decimate you. And bury you in pieces like I did Bambi. You have to be sick in the head to make your niece your Luna!"

"We do not adhere to your archaic rules, I can choose whomever to help lead my pack! You wouldn't be so defensive if I had no merit to what I accuse you of. Admit it!"

I felt Kas wanting to snap his scrawny neck. "Final warning. There is nothing about me that you need to know. If anyone from your band of misfits comes onto my property again without my permission, I will proceed to cover the lands in their blood AND yours! This is not a threat; this is a promise. That is all."

Damien is seething but doesn't physically lash out, he knows better. He has no one at his side like I have Fitz. Instead, he stands as I storm out of his wretched house. "Damien." My final insult as I walk away with Fitz watching my back.

Never trust a wanna be Alpha.

We head back to my property and I hop in the shower before I get comfortable in my bed. Fitz sticks his head in, "Aye, we head out in the morning?" I nod my head and he shut the door.

I was so drained from my meeting with Damien I didn't realize how fast I fell asleep.

I'm standing in nothingness, a black hole or portal. Searching for the smallest bit of light.

Voice: You are a disgrace to your Legacy blood and now you wed the whore of our enemies?

Me: Father?

Voice: I wasted my time conjuring your powers prematurely. You're nothing more than a disappointment.

Me: How'd you do that? Grandma said it was peculiar that I got my powers without having my mate and being marked. She said that maybe I was special.

Voice: Your grandmother was a fool! I bypassed elder law and sent them forth so you can do my bidding.

Then amidst the darkness, he appears, hovering above me. "You are a failure. I should have killed you with your grandmother instead of taking you back with me. I knew you were pathetic, weak!

All my anger flared up, "I knew you killed her, you son of a bitch! She and mom were the only people to care and love me, you were some sick, sadistic, psychopath. I

*won't do it; do you hear me?! This stupid fucking plan of
yours is over. I am finally happy, MY pack is thriving,
and I have my mate who will continue MY legacy, not
yours. I will never tell my child about you. You're a
monster, the kind that gives children nightmares. I will
never be like you."*

*My father leers down at me, "I am a visionary! You'll
never understand but you WILL do my bidding! You are
bound by blood!"*

Suddenly, I found myself on the floor of my room, I
must have tossed and turned myself something awful.
My mind is running rampant, what did he mean I'm
bound by blood? Something is not right, and I feel it
deep down, he might be dead, but I'm not rid of my
father. I must get this under control before something
bad happens to me, Nessa, or the pack, but I don't know
what IT is! Whatever it is now lingers over me like a
dark storm cloud, a sea of impending doom swirling in
my stomach. I tell Fitz to ready the plane now, I've got
to get home.

The nightmares have not only returned, but now I'm
hearing his voice, but there is something very sinister
about it, even more so than when he was alive.

*Voice: You won't attack those inferior Cheshires and
now you wed one of those mutts?! You're a failure to
your bloodline! There will be consequences...whether
you want to or not...you are bound by blood...*

This is not happening at random, it feels like a premonition, a warning, and it left me feeling uneasy.

As I think back over everything, I realize I never forgave my father for what he did. NEVER.

He never explained why he did what he did except to say it was a necessary sacrifice for the pack. Spouting the same power-hungry speech that didn't mean shit initially, he had to pound that logic into me, and I became so worn down I took it on, trying to appease him.

I was unaware he conjured up my powers before he came to take me away. I didn't know he killed my grandmother right before we left for the pack house. He took away the one person who made me feel like I was enough already. What's worse is I fear she saw it coming but didn't warn me.

What was the point of it all? The only outcome is an emotionally scarred and broken man. What a great example of a leader. Is that the example I want to set for my future children? I answered that long ago, absolutely not.

This is all happening right when I discovered Nessa, the pregnancy, and the wedding. Did it start a chain of events? The not knowing is the worst part. My father took an even bigger secret to his grave.

In the morning I took a brisk walk around the grounds trying to understand why these voices started now and why Tavi was able to "disappear". I had no clue and he never openly spoke like Kas does. It felt like the relationship was strictly business even though he was a part of me. It was like I had a rogue living inside me that could attack at any moment.

I had no ill will towards any pack, except Damien's, but this "feud" among the original packs apparently started with my great grandfather and Kayd's great grandfather. But wolves back then were highly territorial, pumped up, adrenaline-fueled animals and this was before the involvement of the Legacies. Now, we've evolved into diplomats and negotiators. Again, I would have never thought to pursue attacking had it not been drilled into my head and I was looking for my father's love and acceptance. I was one fucked up teenager and I would not subject my child to this.

Voice: That child will be cursed, like you, if you do not attack the Cheshire Pack. We will make sure the child suffers...by any means necessary. Attack the mongrels or else! We are watching.

I am on my knees in the woods, with a searing sharp pain behind my eyes. I shake my head out of instinct, but it brings me no relief. Now that voice I am sure was my father and who did he mean by "We?"

My mind was racing a mile a minute. What did he do? I knew the moment he returned from that trip with Uncle Gregory and the more I think about it, the more I know I was right. My father did not come back, something evil disguised as him did.

Only one person knows what happened and I had to find him soon to get insight into what might happen. I thought he was dead, but I discovered from an elder he has been hiding in seclusion. It's time to make a visit and I've tracked him down to a small town called Prince town, about two hours from here.

I inform my leadership that I'm going on a quick trip to visit family. They ask if they need to go. No, I need to seek this truth alone. I pray Nessa doesn't ask where I am, I'm already keeping so much from her.

I hop in the Escalade with my security and in a few hours, I hope to have answers. We hit Princeton city limits and I directed them down a narrow dirt road that ended near a cabin by the lake. The smoke billowing from the chimney lets me know someone was home.

My uncle Gregory was in my life as long as my father, he tried to play the good uncle but there was always something off. He was a Legacy, too, but not as powerful, he also didn't seem to take it seriously and that's probably why my father chose someone else as his Beta instead of his brother.

I knock and wait; I see the curtains ruffle and then I hear shuffling toward the door. It opens and I am face to face with a worn-out-looking version of my father. He looks exhausted and he's lost weight since I last saw him. He gives me a half-smile, "Hey nephew, I suppose you're here to finally kill me?"

WHOA.

"Nice to see you, too, Uncle Gregory. No, I'm not here to kill you. Why would you say something like that?" He signals for me to come in, and I tell my security to wait outside. I sit on the sofa by the fireplace as he sits opposite of me. There are books and papers piled around the living room like he was searching for something. He shuffles papers off the chair and sits down.

"You look awful." Was the only thing I could honestly say, and he chuckled, but it was as emotionless and empty as he was.

"When you harbor as many secrets as I do, you don't find joy in much." He sighs as he rubs his face, his goatee overgrown and peppered in gray. It's as if he's aged 40 years.

"Before we get too deep into the family secrets, how have you been? " I could tell he was stalling, but I obliged him. I needed to know everything he knew.

"Good, I found my mate. We held her Luna ceremony and then got married the following week. Wish you could have been there. Now my life is coming together since I met her." I caught myself smiling.

"Have the voices started?" He said it so nonchalantly that it caught me off guard and I choked.

"H-how do you know about that?"

"I'm afraid they're only going to get worse and more sinister; you are in great danger! Your father was so... obsessed with becoming the Alpha of Alphas. Being a Legacy only amplified it, he thought he was above those who were not. Then he thought he was better than the other Legacy families and, in the end, he traded his soul and other things to make sure that his pack ruled the world. That voice you hear is him, pushing you to implement his plan."

"The only reason I agreed to his plot to conquer was to get his acceptance! I don't want to throw my pack into an unnecessary war, it's stupid and foolish! I will not put my pack in danger, nor my Luna or my child!"

"A child." He states flatly while rubbing his hands, shaking his head, "It's not under your control Christian, your father...did some things in exchange for a guaranteed war. He...he thought you'd be too weak to follow through so he made...some provisions to ensure his plan would succeed."

I grit my teeth, fisting my hands, "What did that bastard do?" I leaned forward, I could see actual fear in his eyes, he swallowed hard. He takes a deep breath, "Christian, know that I have always loved you, you are my nephew, my family and what your father did was vile and reprehensible. He banished me before he died so that I wouldn't be able to warn you. I was stuck in this cabin by a force field until he died."

"Why didn't you come after he died?! To warn me!"

"I-I was so guilt-ridden and afraid. I wasn't sure if he had already influenced you or not or if you would kill me on sight! I hoped maybe that since he died suddenly that it nullified the agreement, the deal he made with the devil."

All I couldn't think was, what had he done?!

"Stop stalling! What did he do to me?!" Kas was growling in my ear, he was riled up and pacing ready to break through, but I needed to know this dark family secret.

Uncle Gregory plops down on the couch, heavily. I sit back cautiously to ease his mind. The air is thick with tension as he sighs once more.

"Christian, one day your father and I took a trip to a witch doctor a few towns over from here. I know you saw us arguing before the doors closed and he blocked the link to avoid you hearing any part of the conversation. He was adamantly convinced after watching you practice that you wouldn't be strong enough to carry out his plan. He set his sights on plan B..."

Papa Ezekiel's Cottage, some years back

Gregory: What are we doing here, Tomas?

Tomas: Solidifying the longevity of my pack, by any means necessary!

Gregory: What does that mean? What are you going to do?

Tomas: Win.

Older gentleman enters the room

Papa Ezekiel: Alpha Grey to what do I owe the pleasure?

Tomas: Papa Ezekiel I come to you to sacrifice whatever it takes to guarantee my pack reigns supreme. Money, gold, whatever! I will give it to you to make this happen.

Papa Ezekiel stands in front of his altar and mixes a potion. His back towards them as he pulls various bottles to pour into the copper bowl

Ezekiel: Anything, you say? You know that you must make a great sacrifice for whatever you please. I will ensure whatever you want in exchange for two things: your immortal soul and you to be subservient as long as the spell is binding.

Drops in an herb and a green smoke billows from the bowl

Tomas: Done!

Gregory: WHAT?! Your soul?! You can never go to heaven if you are stuck under his control. You would never see mama and papa or any of our family in the great beyond, are you that power-hungry that you are willing to never see us again?!

Ezekiel: Listen carefully to your brother because what he says is true. There is no going back from this; only my death sets you free and know that you will be condemned to Hell for entering this deal. Think wise but think fast...the potion is almost complete.

Tomas is salivating as he watches him put the ingredients together, those that could open the floodgates to achieving his life's long work.

Tomas: Done.

Gregory: Tom-

Tomas holds his hand up

Tomas: I said done. One more stipulation, if I fail in my lifetime, pass this down to my son with a precursor that his sorcerer takes over and carries out the plan with or without his consent. And carry it forth throughout the future generations. This MUST happen, we WILL be on top! My sacrifice will not be in vain. It is my will, make it so.

Ezekiel: Then so be it.

Gregory: Are you fucking mad?!

Ezekiel: He has chosen and I have made the potion that will bind him, his son, so on and so forth until the task is achieved.

Gregory: Tomas, don't subject Christian to this! He should be allowed to live his life as he sees fit NOT how you want it to happen. He is...

Tomas: WEAK AND USELESS! He isn't fit to carry the pack to greater heights. Greatness requires sacrifice!

Papa Ezekiel hands the bowl over with the murky black liquid to Tomas, who stares into the thick concoction. He drinks it down with no remorse. His body glows amber and his eyes flash from black to amber. A sinister chuckle slips his lips

Ezekiel: It is done, my pet. Now you harness the power, but use it wisely, the power is not linear it can come around full circle. Now that you are under my power you will carry out my first task. You must find an amulet in your mother's cottage; it harnesses great power I can use.

Tomas bows

Tomas: I will retrieve it for you.

Gregory lunges at Tomas, but Tomas flings him against the wall with the flick of his wrist, knocking the wind from him. He groans in pain.

Tomas: Apologies for my weakling of a brother. He doesn't have my drive; that's why I was chosen as Alpha and not him. He'll always be second fiddle and probably won't make much of himself other than riding my coattails.

inhales I can feel the infinite power!

Ezekiel: Good, my pet, when you return with what I ask, you will be on your way to your desires.

Tomas looks surprised momentarily, then nods. He picks up his brother with ease and leaves Papa Ezekiel's cottage

Back to the present:

What did I listen to? Like what in the actual fuck?!

"You're telling me that I'm cursed?! That I'm forced to do the bidding of my deranged dead father, and that this could possibly be passed on to my child?"

Kas wants out, he wants to rip my uncle apart, but I can't let my anger consume me, I am not my father, and I push Kas down deep. My uncle's not to blame, my father is.

My psychotic, screwed up, willing to sacrifice himself, and apparently me, for power, father.

I need to figure out how powerful Tavi has gotten in the shadows, I can't let him carry out the plan.

I couldn't even continue this conversation, I needed to get back home. I turn to leave when he screams out, "When I came to, he had locked me inside this place with a force field. He knew I would try to protect you. You have to find a solution before it's too late, it probably already is!"

The hell it is.

I slam the door and tell them to hightail it back to pack grounds immediately.

I was supposed to spend time with my wife, but I don't even know how safe that is. I curse my father's name, hoping he's burning in the Hell he created.

I had another vision on my way home, this one more disturbing than the last one. I recognized the strip bar and I was sitting at our table. It was me, but it wasn't me. My mannerisms were off and there was a certain negative energy surrounding me. It was like I was hearing my father's voice in my body:

*"It's bad enough I sense her on their pack land, she's affiliated...affiliated with my enemies but...this could work to my advantage. My precious little mate doesn't have to know everything. She needs to be on my side when I lay out my plan of attack on the "great" Cheshire pack. Her love binds her no matter how close she is to Luna Kamari and if she fights it, I'll reject her, and it will kill her. She'll be too in love to go against me though, this **WILL** go as planned no matter how long it takes. "*

I would never speak about my Nessa like that, nor would I ever think about attacking Kayden unprovoked. It's like he wanted me to see how he would have done it if he were me. It made my skin crawl as I tried to shake myself out of that nightmare. I won't let him win; I won't let him take anything from me!

I link everyone to meet me in my office when I pass the gate and head up the driveway. I slammed my office door growling at the horrific revelation. I thought I had to worry about my external enemies and now I have one internally like a ticking time bomb.

Judging by their faces they recognize there's a big problem.

"What are we up against? I feel a fight coming, who is it? Damien? Brenner? Some pack in the East? We are ready to wage war against our enemy, whoever it is!" Fitz sounds strong and confident; little did he know...

I sigh as I sit at my desk, tenting my fingers. "The problem is much bigger than we could ever imagine. The dark cloud that is threatening to pour is coming from within."

"We got another spy. Who is it?!" Kellan jumps up slamming his fists on the table.

I hold my hand up, "That dark cloud is me, I am the threat to our pack."

Fitz stands with his brows furrowed, "I don't understand, Chris. How are you a threat to the pack?"

I stand and perch against the front of my desk and sigh loudly, "Apparently, my father made a dark pact with a witch doctor for a chance to overthrow the Cheshires or the Legacies, in exchange he gave up his soul and cursed me to go through with this plan. He empowered Tavi to take over and I don't know how to stop him. It's me. I am my pack's enemy."

If you could see their confused faces. "Well, he is a part of you, how do you know he's not listening now?"

"I'm sure he is or has been, but he has given me radio silence for a while now. Now that he knows I know, I fear the attack is imminent and I need to take drastic measures. Fitz, you're going to lead the pack in my absence."

"What?! Where are you going? We should come up with a plan together!"

"There's no time! You are going to chain me up in the dungeon until we figure out how to kill Papa Ezekiel or break this curse. If he dies my father is free of him and hopefully, the curse is lifted but I can't put all my eggs in one basket. If we can't kill him, we're going to have to find another way."

"Ummm," Kirin raises his hand, "What about Nessa?"

Yeah, that's going to be fun. Nothing like a crisis to force you to tell your mate all the secrets and lies you've held in for more than a year. I'm more terrified of her than whatever this unknown is but I need her.

"I will tell her everything after we finish here. We all know I am screwed for lying to her and not telling her about my status, but she can help you figure it out. What worries me is she's going to want to help." I groan, rubbing my face as I link her to come to my office. "Stay." That's all I say as I await the firestorm that is my wife.

She knocks and I tell her to come in.

Before I say anything, a flash of white streaks across my eyes and I hear my father's sinister laugh; he whispers:

The whore carries a half-breed bastard. Weaker than his father. Your efforts are too little too late...

I want to scream shut up, but I shake my head and come back to the present where she's already in front of me. I'm trying not to react to my father's vicious name-calling.

"Sit please, my darling. I don't have much time, but I need you to understand that I didn't do this intentionally. I came to my senses, but I fear now it may be too late."

Your efforts are too little too late...

I did everything wrong, giving him what he wanted. FUCK!

Fear, that's all I see in her eyes. "What did you do, Christian?" She didn't sound concerned or scared but she was mad. It was the spark to the kindling that could very well end up as a bonfire or explosion once she knew the

173

entire truth. She sat back and crossed her legs waiting for me, the silence was deafening.

I fall to my knees in front of her, to be close and to admit defeat. I take her hands and she leans forward.

"Nessa, I love you so much. I don't know why I agreed to this plan or why I almost let his insane ramblings influence the way I run my pack. I was a boy wanting the love of his father but...now I realize I would never pressure my child like he did to me."

"You're rambling, get to the lie, Christian Evan. I know you think I might leave or reject you, but I am telling you that this will not break us. Just tell me."

She squeezes my hand and I feel better.

"I'm a hybrid."

Her eyes start to well, the heartbreak is devastating. "Why would you lie about that? Do you know how hard it is to be a hybrid, to feel accepted?!"

"Because...I'm no ordinary hybrid. I'm a Legacy, Nessa, an Amber Legacy and in my father's eyes all other families were our enemies and so Kam...was my adversary by default."

She drops my hands and stands up to put some distance between us. "Kam would NEVER do anything to you or this pack! She is the most peaceful person on this planet and my best friend! How dare you?! All she was obsessed with was finding true love. She wouldn't give two shits about another pack or overthrowing them or any of that male chauvinistic bullshit! She only uses her witch to protect what and who she loves and that includes me!" She paces the floor while staring into my soul, her eyes flicker black then silver.

They are all pissed at me.

"I-I know that. It was what was drilled into me repeatedly and I started to believe it, I wanted my father's acceptance! I was willing to believe any crackpot theory he told me, and I agreed...to take down the Cheshire Pack, overthrow them and take the top spot..."

"WHAT?!" She laughs but it is not a comedic laugh. The fellas slowly back away until they are closer to the door.

Lucky them.

"So how did you feel about finding your mate in the pack of you 'enemies'? First, you go after Kam because she's a Legacy and now you go after Kayd because of his pack rank?! Was I a disappointment to you? Sleeping with the enemy! Huh?!" She was irate, I would never cheapen her like that. "You could never disappoint me. I was relieved! You were there for a reason, to make some sense of this. I realized long ago I don't want to pursue this, I can't."

She hugged me and it surprised me when three seconds ago she was ready to rip me open or incinerate me.

"That's great!" She looks at my face, "Why do I feel there's a 'but' to that statement?"

I sat down in the seat she was in and then placed her on my lap. "My father sold his soul to a witch doctor named Papa Ezekiel in exchange for the power to put his plan into action and if he couldn't...I would be forced to do it on his behalf."

"But...how..."

"It's Tavi, my sorcerer. Papa Ezekiel gave him the power to separate and take over to carry it out. He's been missing for days and all I get are flash visions and nightmares about the carnage. I can't let him out, I need to lock myself away until Papa Ezekiel is rid of. I'm going to have them put me in the dungeon and shackled heavily until we figure it out. Please, don't try to reason with me, it's because of me we're in this predicament. I will fight tooth and nail to keep him at bay, Fitz will run the pack and maybe you could help find an answer."

I grab her hands, holding them down. "You can't visit me Nessa, I'm already super uneasy to tell you this because I know you want to help, I'll die if something happens to you or our pup."

Her lip quivers and she places her fingers on my chin, then she smacks my chest, "Kam fought that bitch and her ex while pregnant with twins and I can, too! And if you think differently, you are sadly mistaken, dear husband of mine. You lied to me and hid your Legacy status, we'll deal with that later, but the safety of this pack is critical now. We need to…"

I'm elated, but that joy is short-lived as my knees buckle, I grit my teeth straining and struggling to keep control. I have the urge to lash out, the intense hatred coming through is unbearable. "RAWR! He's coming, we have to go, NOW!"

The twins shift into their wolves in case Tavi can force me to shift. We hurry out of the house, guided by the light of the moon, and down into the dungeon. Giving my security guards a quick rundown of what is happening. What they didn't see or feel was that Kas was in combative mode, growling into the darkness of my mind. He knew the war on our sanity had begun.

K: Kas will do best but don't know how strong evil witch is.

C: I trust you, Kas. You're my front line.

Then a flash of light and another sharp pain shoots across the back of my head and I see Tavi's form coming closer from the darkness, he's surrounded by white light and lightning. I fall to my knees; the pain is excruciating.

"Chain me now! We're out of time!" I'm gritting my teeth so hard they may shatter but it keeps me from screaming out.

"Chris!"

"Stay back Nessa! I...I love you...AHHHHH!"

The world goes black for a split second and when I come to, I'm lying in darkness. It sounds like a low echo or like I'm in a cave. My head is pounding and my vision is blurry. I can't focus because it's dark.

What just happened?

"Uh human, we have BIG problem." I look over to see Kas beside me, his eyes glowing in the darkness to include his fur, which means...

"Fuck! He got out!"

"I tried to fight but he threw Kas against wall hard. I black out. Kas sorry."

"No, you did what you could and gave me enough time to lock myself away. Goddess help them. Especially my girl."

Chris collapsed as they finished shackling him down. His cries of pain send me into panic.

"Chris!" I run towards him, but Fitz picks me up to stop me. "No! He's not in control. My wolf is growling...stand back." He's right, both my girls are agitated. They've gone into protective mode to keep my baby safe.

He's still on his knees with his head down but a glow begins to appear around him, it's the Amber Legacy glow. Much like Kam's Violet glow but the atmosphere of the room was all wrong.

The laugh emitted was ominous, it was sinister, downright evil but most importantly...it was not Christian. He yanks at the chains binding him, but they don't budge much, they look to be industrial quality and the posts are at least 50 feet deep. It's standard practice for packs who still implement dungeons. I noticed they limit the movement of his hands which was smart, he wouldn't be able to cast certain spells without the proper movement but what was more worrisome is the types of spells he may know.

"You think you can hold me?! Weak and pathetic like he is, he would have never carried out a successful attack, but I will! You're all expendable, I don't need any of you, especially some whore and fetus."

Calliope rushed forward so fast I couldn't stop her after he insulted us. Now there are two powerful entities in this small space. The wind was whipping my straight hair around furiously. The guys were shielding their faces as the dust and dirt swirled around us.

"It would be in your best interest not to insult me nor my child. Whether you are a part of our husband or not, I will not tolerate disrespect!"

He sneered at me, "A Luna is just the Alpha's prized whore!" It took everything to hold Calliope back from torching our husband's body.

N: Calliope don't! It's not him talking but his sorcerer, we have to find a way to separate him!

She roars out her frustration. I heard distant thunder simultaneously.

C: Let's go before he pushes me into I-don't-give-a-fuck territory. Call Kam and then Miss Ren, she might come up with something in her infinite wisdom before I incinerate that disrespectful motherfu...

I agreed as she stormed into the depths of my mind unleashing a fury of expletives. I watched my husband's body flail and thrash around. Tavi contorts his body so harshly and inhumanely it looks painful, but I know he's deep within the recesses of his mind, but I have to look away.

"Fitz, set up 24-hour surveillance, he is NEVER to be out of anyone's sight, I don't care if he is shackled down, he might still be able to conjure. He's not going to show his hand to his enemies. Also, make sure the security cameras are always recording and amplify security around the grounds until further notice. I know I'll have to address the pack soon but first I need options."

"Yes, Luna. If you need anything, please call on us."

I need my husband. I squeak to myself.

It pains me to watch that monster affect my Alpha. He almost broke free while Chris was trying to reassure me. I know Chris would never hurt me, quite the opposite, but Tavi he's a complete mystery. In fact, I just found out he existed! I have my security outside of my bedroom as I go in and pace the floor while dialing Kam.

"Nessa, hey! What's that sound I hear?"

"I put you on speakerphone, it's me making a divot on the floor from pacing. Kam there's so much shit going on, I don't know what to do! I-I need help!"

I'm crying profusely after my admission. It hits me like a brick wall. Kam requests a video chat. I see the worry on her face when she sees her broken friend. She was ready to pack her bags.

"Kayd, come in here!" He appears behind Kam and he immediately tries to read my body language. "Okay, now tell us what's going on."

"Hey, Kayd."

"Hey Nes, what's wrong?"

Suddenly it was like the dam burst, "My husband lied to me, he's a Legacy, Kam! An Amber Legacy," I watch her gasp as she slapped her hand over her mouth. "He told me that the reason he kept it a secret was that, for his father to accept him, he agreed to wage war... against the Cheshires or the Legacies. He decided against it, but his father cursed him to carry out the plan through his sorcerer. He's chained in the dungeon right now!"

I hear Kayd growl and Kam calming him. I knew he wouldn't be happy about that; I was afraid they would cut all ties with me. I needed to fix what I could. "I'm sorry! The only reason he's down there is that he warned us and we got him locked down before his sorcerer appeared. What do I do Kam, everything is so screwed up!"

Kam sighs, "That is a lot. We don't blame you for this Nes, he kept it from you and honestly, you're going to think this is crazy, but he probably should have. You are a temperamental monster when you are raging, you could have made it worse. You would have waged war against your husband."

"She's right, Nes." Kayd interrupts, "You are the most important thing to him, especially now that you're pregnant. He's going to fight hard to get back to you. Do you have a plan? " I throw my hands up in defeat. "No. He said his father went to a witch doctor named Papa Ezekiel, forked over his soul and Chris' sorcerer's power to him. What do I do now?! I can't do this without him."

I couldn't stop crying if I tried. I had to face this alone because my mate was the problem.

"I'm so sorry you guys, I-I didn't know!"

"Don't worry about that, nothing's changed between us, you're still family. Now, what are your first steps?"

"I need to know how powerful his sorcerer is. A witch and a Legacy witch are two different levels that's why I called to ask you what I am up against."

Kam fidgets nervously, "A Legacy anything is powerful, but he is not as powerful as me, but he's still very dangerous. You'll need to find a way to break that pact, that's the only thing I can think of right now. Say the word, I'll come out there!"

"No, you just had the twins, this is my problem."

Kayd shook his head, "No. This is OUR problem, Nes. You may be a part of their pack, but you will always be family. You're like a sister to me, an annoying little sister. I agree Kam shouldn't travel but I can be there if you need me to."

"As helpful as it might sound, I think it would be the exact opposite, he would be enraged knowing his 'mortal enemy' was on his land and in his house. He could get rid of Chris permanently and I can't risk it. But you could ask the pack historians for advice, maybe they know something we don't. I'll ask Miss Ren, my Luna instructor, to see if she knows anything. She is divinely favored and has decades of wisdom.

I look into the eyes of my family, "We love you Nessa, whatever you need from us, we're here. I guarantee you he is not going to give up easily. He loves his wife and his child."

I burst out in tears, "His son. I was going to tell him today, Kam. We're having a little boy!" I rub my tiny bump and smile with tears as Kam tears up, too. I found out a few hours before he called me to his office. Like her pregnancy, mine will be accelerated.

"I can't wait to meet my precious little nephew but first, we'll have a meeting with our historians, and I will call my parents, too. They obviously know more about Legacies. We love you Nes, stay strong."

I could only wave. I clean my face and wait for Miss Ren, hoping she can help. I hear the lightest tap on my door. I sniffle before I answer, "Come in."

Miss Ren walks in and the door closes behind her. Her tiny frame walks over and she places her hands on my face like a grandmother does and I let the tears fall, it's cathartic.

"Hush child, I know, I know. You will get through this. I made a stop down there and he's a nasty creature filled with hate, but it is not our Alpha. He's stronger than his sorcerer, he is their lifeline, and he cannot kill him, he needs him."

"But he can harm him and that's what I'm afraid of. Inflicting pain on my husband and him becoming a shell of his former self. I got to find a way to break this curse, Miss Ren. Do you know who Papa Ezekiel is?"

She hissed the second his name spilled from my lips, "Ooh, child! Do not speak his name, it's like calling a demon! He is a powerful entity, but he is not immortal even though he has tried to negotiate with the darkness. I told Tomas not to visit him when he sought my guidance. He lied to me about going and doomed this child! I'm so disappointed in him. I'll need my sisterhood for this." She lifts my chin, "Be strong child. Rest up for you and that strong healthy boy growing inside you." I was shocked as she smiled, "I can also see bits of the future. Do a simple protective spell before you go to sleep and in the morning, we'll hatch a plan." She kisses my head and I feel comforted but sad knowing my husband was suffering, that I wouldn't feel him lying next to me cradling my bump. I wanted to spill *his* blood in the name of my husband.

N: Calliope, did you...

C: Protective spell intact for the entire house. Dalila and I will take shifts monitoring the situation. I'm...I'm sorry I didn't see this coming.

Shocked again, because Calliope doesn't do human feelings such as love or anything, but she felt guilty.

N: We all wish we could have stopped this, it's not your fault. Let's focus on the goal of getting our Alpha back. He's got a big responsibility growing in here.

C: You are already so nurturing for the tiny hybrid. Will he be half Legacy, half werewolf or will he divide into thirds?

She had a point; I didn't know if his Legacy sorcerer would cancel out my silver witch. I guess we wait and see. The twins would be a guiding principle as they grow. I would expect something similar to happen with my son.

N: I don't know Calliope; I want my family together and a sense of normalcy.

I lie down, about to doze off, when there is a knock.

"Come in."

I see Kirin and Kellan come in, they look weary but smile, trying to keep my hopes up. Kirin is carrying a tray, I see a glass of milk and a simple sandwich with lemon cookies, my current craving.

"Hey, we're making sure you eat something before bed."

I take half a sandwich to nibble on. "Thanks...how is it down there?"
I saw them both flinch. "Honestly, it's not pretty, but we're taking care of it, don't you worry." I stared a hole through him and he realized that's not something you should say.

"What I meant to say is you need to take care of yourself, please. When he returns, he'll check you from head to toe to make sure you're okay."

"As I plan to do with him! Please, be gentle with him, I know he's fighting from the inside, but he only has one body." I felt my throat tighten as I looked away to avoid crying. They hug me and I take a few more bites before exhaustion overwhelms me.

Back in the dungeon:

Tavi continues to thrash around while chained down to the floor as Chris instructed. He growls in Fitz's direction. His Amber Legacy burned like an inferno from his eyes. Fitz sits in a chair directly in front but out of his reach.

"Don't do this Tavarious, Chris doesn't want this, and you know it!"

His vicious growl echoed in the dungeon, "We are contracted by blood! We are bound to annihilate our enemy. They WILL burn to cinders!"

Fitz checks the time and scrubs his face, it was 2 a.m. before this, he was dealing with pack business and now, he was Alpha by default until this situation was resolved. One guard comes in, bowing. "Alpha, you need rest, I will take over."

That dark, malevolent laugh echoes louder in the hollow room, "Do not disgrace that title when you address a peasant! He is an inferior Alpha compared to me! Once

I'm free I'll rule this pack on my own. You'll merely be an imprint on the wall after I hurl a fireball to consume you!" He made the hand gesture as best he could but could not give full motion which was a relief.

Fitz concedes, "Be vigilant, he doesn't let up. I'll be back at 7 a.m. sharp." He resigns to his room to rest. Soon they must inform the pack of what has befallen their Alpha. He silently worried about his best friend's well-being.

"This is bullshit! How can he block me from control?!" I beat my fists against the dark walls of my mind and it echoed back. I hear Tavi laugh at my downfall, basking in his temporary power. He was no better being chained up, but he was out there, and I was in here.

Kas stares at me with a stoic look, "Kas told you he was up to no good. When we free, say I told you so, but not now. Need plan."

I'm fuming, scared, confused, and disappointed at the predicament my father put me in without my permission. I should have made it my mission to never be like him, but I was trying to be the "perfect" son. But I was never good enough in his eyes.

I now wondered was my father's death really an accident. I believe Papa Ezekiel collected his soul prematurely and my mom was a casualty. She loved him more than anything, I could see it in her eyes. Whenever they were together, she would gaze up at him lovingly as he spoke. But sometimes, I could see the pain in her eyes when she didn't always agree with his decisions. She never spoke up. It may be her gentle nature or maybe she feared for her life. Now that I knew about his deal, I was even more enraged at losing my mother, to hell with him.

bzzz bzzz bzzz

Ughhh, I was praying everything was a horrific night terror caused by my weird food cravings until my hand slapped the cold side next to me and the tears well up. Hopelessness lingering over me like a dark cloud. I make a heart-breaking self-confession, "I can't do this alone."

C: You will never be alone. We will always protect you. Remain strong, you are Luna of this pack, and you need to tell them about the last 24 hours. You'll need more hands to help find a solution.

Reluctantly, I get dressed. Relaying this will not be easy especially since I'll be fighting back my emotions. I dressed in all black, an off-the-shoulder sweater and black ripped jeans. I wore black high tops instead of my signature heels. I know my eyes are puffy and swollen, I look so tired without my makeup, but the wall was long gone, I would not hide my emotions.

I hear Fitz summon everyone outside and they are in formation by the time I walk over. I could see the concern on their faces and hear the whispers.

"Good morning, Luna Nessa." They all say with sadness not knowing how to step into this unknown situation.

I try to clear my throat without an audible sob. Fitz gives me a half hug. I inhaled deeply, "Umm, you may be wondering why we called you here this morning and why Alpha Grey isn't here. He...umm..." I wipe a wayward tear and I can see the concern amplify.

Fitz steps forward in line with me, "Alpha Grey is, for lack of a better word, in trouble, and we need everyone's help to find a solution. He recently found out about a curse placed upon him by his father. He is an Amber Legacy descendant and his sorcerer has gained control and wants to viciously attack those he believes are his enemies."

Audible gasps rang out and the whispers continued. Fitz continues as I turn away to pull myself together. Even hearing it shatters me all over again, when will it end?

"He has been locked away in the dungeon and no one is permitted except those working security. He is okay, he made sure to put the pack first when he voluntarily chained himself up. In the meantime, our Luna has allowed me to step in temporarily until our fearless leader is back and stronger than before. What we need from you is to be vigilant and if you have knowledge of witchcraft, magic, or folklore please see me."

I see a sea of heads nodding, there were quite a few people from the older generation and fewer from the generation before. I was staring at a lot of wisdom, hoping we could find a solution.

"Please also help our Luna during this difficult time as well, she...she's…" I put my hand on his shoulder to stop him. "What he is trying to say is that Alpha Grey is going to be a father and that's why I desperately need him back, I need him home to take care of the next leader of this pack. Thank you, everyone."

I sigh heavily as they disperse but I notice a few ladies are waiting on the sideline as I turn towards the house.

They bow, "Luna Nessa, we are so very sorry to hear what has happened to our beloved Alpha but so excited for your present state. We want to offer our services to you personally if you need anything. We won't take no for an answer. We will link periodically to check up on you, just know you don't and won't do this alone, ever." They wrap me up in the warmest hug I have ever received and for a moment, I was okay.

Then I heard a blood-curdling scream coming from the dungeon and I made my way quickly, the screams turned into screeches and yelling and then I could hear him audibly curse someone's name.

"You senile old bat! Do you think holy water is going to harm me?! You're as foolish as you are ignorant! I am powered by a great and powerful witch doctor! One ask and I can have him torch you to cinders!"

I see Miss Ren and a circle of elderly ladies surrounding Chris, his shirt was open, and his chest was marked with a symbol in what looks to be charcoal. The same charcoal was used to create a pentagram and other symbols on the ground.

"Hush up, demon! This was to see how vulnerable you are. You're not as powerful as you think, you're a pawn, a minion. Tell your Master we want to cut a deal. Free Alpha Christian from a tie he did not make, a bond he did not agree to tell him to name his terms."

His eyes darkened and a smirk formed across his face, "Would you be willing to sacrifice yourself for him? Hmm...a soul for a soul? You could be a formidable asset if you submit to him."

I had heard enough, I burst through, "No! Please don't! Chris wouldn't want you to do this!"

She catches me before I go tumbling to the ground. The ladies remain in their places, softly chanting.

"Although he tries to hide it, I can feel him struggling physically and internally. You shouldn't be here for the sake of our future Alpha. Please, child, go!"

"No, not if you want to give your soul to him, please, there has to be another way!"

She smiles warmly at me, "There is my child, I would never trade my soul to that monster, besides he hasn't heard from his "master" since he took over. This is the residual work of Tomas. If Ezekiel is behind this, he would gloat by now, but I'll keep an eye open to see if he appears. I may have a solution but, to make this work, I will need to speak with Gregory. He may be the key to ending the curse."

"W-who is Gregory?"

I felt a shift in the environment and suddenly everything stopped and went deathly silent. I feel like I stopped breathing. He was quiet, his body limp, his head slumped over, and his breathing seemed to regulate. He shook his head, groaning.

"Nes...Nessa?"

"Chris? Chris! Is that really you?"

Oh, please let this be him, I need to know he's okay.

When he looks up, he locks his eyes on me and I know. I move towards him, but he shakes his head furiously. "No, stay back! I don't trust him... near you... I know you're worried, I'm okay my darlin'. I love you and I'm coming back...to you. GO NOW! Ahhh..."

evil chuckle "That's enough of that sappy dribble. See how pathetic he is? Weak...over a woman...pitiful." He spat at me.

I don't want to harm him physically, instead I lash out verbally, "Shut up! You aren't even a person! You're just an entity, a part that needs him to be whole. Without him you are nothing and so help me I will get my husband back. Chris, I love you so much!" I choke out before I run away, completely shattered.

"...Chris, I love you so much." I wanted to profess how I loved her so much but before I could say anything he yanked me back into the darkness. I hit hard enough to knock the wind out of me causing me to cough and gasp for air. He's trying to break my spirit when he fueled my determination. There's got to be a way out of this nightmare.

I feel hopeless and useless, the inability to help is gut-wrenching. I hate this! I let my tears fall onto his pillow until my phone rings. It's a video call from Kam. I don't even bother sitting up. I let her see the truth.

"Oh Nes, sweetie."

"I don't like feeling like this. He's my mate, my husband, I'm supposed to protect him as much as he does me…"

"I know and you will. We need to approach this carefully; we can't react emotionally."

Says the one who took on her enemy while pregnant with my niece and nephew, but she was right. That slut was nothing special and John Michael was hopped up on steroids with a small dick complex. This was a magical being.

"Kam, he was back for a moment and he was so worried about me...or us. All he cared about was…" I rub my stomach. "Him."

Kayd comes behind Kam and then she pans out more to reveal her mother seated and her father standing. They looked like an elegant family portrait.

I try to pull myself together, sitting up and wiping away my tears. "Mr. and Mrs. Remington, it's so nice to see you again." I sniffle as they give me a pity smile.

"Nessa, my sweet girl, it's good to see you, not under these circumstances, but we are here to help. I know you know a bit about the Legacy line from Kam and her experience. It's true there is some animosity between the families but mostly we have kept the peace. Although Alpha Tomas may have thought we were naive about his intentions, we were always a few steps ahead, surrounding and protecting our baby girl."

I hear a knock and Miss Ren peeks around the corner and I wave her in. "Everybody, this is my Luna instructor Miss Ren. Miss Ren, this is King Malcolm Remington and Queen Melody Lee-Remington of the Violet Legacies. Alpha Kayden and Princess Kamari Miller of the Cheshire Pack. My family."

She does a little curtsy with her bow, "Oh my, it is a great honor to meet you all, I have heard so many good things. I apologize for interrupting."

King Malcolm smiles, "Not a problem, I am glad to see someone there to help my bonus daughter through this situation. What I was going to tell you, is there is an ancient removal ceremony; it has been executed only twice, once among the Jade Legacy and unfortunately, once within the Violets. I suppose every family would have its day, now it's yours."

Great. Queen Melody squeezes his hand as he continues, "This is a fatal flaw among the Legacies that we are too ashamed to talk about. What happens is a Legacy child goes mad with power, wanting it all. Willing to destroy the world to obtain it. They seek out someone who promises them absolute supremacy. They are so drunk on attaining control they verbally agree and in the Violet case, he unleashed an attack on the Legacy families and almost won, too. The bloodshed was extensive as Jade and Amber helped us against one of our very own. His sorcerer was extremely powerful, we lost one of our elders who had found out about the removal ceremony to stop him. He was able to tell us that to complete the spell, another Legacy would have to sacrifice themselves to break the curse, but at the same time, the one affected would lose their Legacy power entirely. One would be left with only his wolf while the other...would die."

I looked over to see Kam in utter shock, she was learning something new about her family all the time. The time away kept her from discovering that being a Legacy isn't all it's cracked up to be. The secrets, the lies, absolute betrayal, it was like a soap opera and now I was smack dab in my own.

Miss Ren clears her throat, "I was sincerely hoping we hadn't come to the same conclusion, but he is correct. We tested magic mirrors, binding, spell refracting, and a few curse-breaking rituals but whatever Papa Ezekiel has conjured up is more powerful and complicated to be reversed by common methods. I recall both breaches and the toll it took on the families and packs. I was there for the Jade cleansing and the damage was irreversible and we can't have that, our Alpha needs to bounce back stronger than before. The coven and I have been working on a spell to cast at the same time as the extraction to minimize the damage. King Remington, like you, I have seen the ritual performed and I won't lie to you Vanessa, it isn't pretty."

My breathing hitches, there's a chance when he returns, he won't be the same and it guts me. I cry into my hands and she wraps her arms around me. "Don't you go crying yet, child, we have a very powerful coven and protection is our specialty, it's the extraction that will be hardest. We need to find Gregory and convince him to make the great sacrifice."

I look up and everyone's silent, "His life? Who is he?"

"Gregory is Christian's uncle and also a Legacy, he is the key to breaking his father's deal with Papa Ezekiel."

"Papa Ezekiel?!" King Remington exclaimed, "That's who charmed the other Legacies to give up their souls. This is not a freak occurrence; he's been targeting the Legacies for generations. He's come close but not as close as he seems to be now, you need to find his..."

A knock interrupts him and my leadership appears, I wave them over and introduce everyone and catch them up on our discussion.

Fitz links our security guards to find out who took Chris to see his Uncle. They tell us they can take us to his cottage, that's a couple of hours away.

Good, I can get there and back before dark.

Fitz reads me like a book, "No way, Nes, I'm trying to avoid certain death here. Either I or the twins will go and convince him."

Everyone nods and I sigh utterly frustrated. The room is feeling crowded and I just want his arms around me.

I can't take this; I need some air!

"You guys can continue; I need to get out of here. Alone!" I state harshly because I saw them try to follow. I allow one of my bodyguards to follow from a distance. I made my way toward the cliff. I assured my very concerned bodyguard I would not jump. I stand there letting the salt-infused air hit me as I try to wrap my head around it, this was only our first year. What if he doesn't come back the same, could I still love him? Of course, I would love any semblance of him who loved me back.

I watch the waves crash against the cliffs, the roar is loud and drowns out the sound of my heart breaking. I rub my stomach, "Hi, little one. I promise mama will do everything in her power to get your daddy back. He needs me and I am going to do whatever it takes to help him so he...can watch you grow and become as powerful as him." I sniffle and then I feel a presence because both my girls go into a combative stance.

I turned to see a rather haggard man who looked like an older version of Chris. He had warm brown skin and the same mesmerizing eyes with his hair pulled back into a ponytail. His eyes met mine and followed down to where my hand lay on my stomach.

My security guard hadn't moved from his post, he didn't react like he was an intruder. It was as if he knew who he was. The stranger says nothing as he steps closer and now, he is mere feet from me. He stared at my stomach; his breathing labored as the tears fell.

"Another generation in front of me. I never thought he'd allow me to see the day. And you...are more beautiful than Chris described. I knew his Luna would complete him and fight for him. Everything my sister-in-law tried to do for my brother."

He wouldn't look me in the eye and in that moment, it clicked, "You're... Gregory...his uncle." I can tell he wants to console me and hug me. But he was fighting with himself and ultimately decided not to.

I try to comfort him verbally, let him know that I am not judging him. "Come on, let's get you something to eat." He follows as I link that Gregory was already here. The conversation became almost like white noise, static, a barrage of questions I didn't have answers to. He kindly responded that he could still access the pack link. The conversation trickled down to complete radio silence and I chuckled. I didn't know the whole story, but he could very well be the key to saving my Alpha's life.

"Stop this Tavi, they're not going to let us go! IT IS FOOLISH TO CONTINUE!" I shout with every fiber of my being, draining my energy. I lie helplessly on the ground, breathing heavily. I know he can hear me as I would hear him in my thoughts.

"The longer I'm in control, the weaker you become. I will take over your being and I'll toss that mangy mutt in a cage for all eternity."

The laughter that erupts sounds like one of victory, but I would rather die together than unleash him onto the world. I hate to even think about leaving Nessa, but as far as I can see...my only out maybe death.

"We might have to die to save my family." I say to Kas.

Nessa

"Come inside, Gregory, please." He stands nervously at the doorway, watching as the people passing by gasp and whisper. They make themselves scarce quickly after I told them it was impolite to stare.

I hear a commotion coming from the direction of my room, it sounds like a stampede when I see Fitz charging down the stairs. He is not happy, and that is an understatement.

"You yellow-belly son of a bitch! You hid like a spineless coward while your nephew suffers and now look where we are! You're as at fault as your psycho brother!" The twins are having a hard time holding him back as his wolf scratches the surface, his eyes black as coal as he lets out his Beta roar.

"Fitz, stop! This isn't helping! I could lose my husband!" I screeched, which stopped everyone cold. I lean against the nearby post rubbing my stomach but refusing anyone near me.

"No, he's right. I am a coward, I tried to stop Tomas and failed. After he knocked me unconscious, I was at home and scared to face whatever it was that was now controlling my brother. I deserve to be berated and shunned, I didn't protect my nephew and now he suffers because of it. I am here to make it right. I am here... to die for my nephew."

I push myself back up to standing, "You know about the ritual?"

"I did some research on ancient Legacy history and rituals while my brother locked me away. A harboring evil lurking in the shadows has always been in the books, it was predicted long ago. The only thing they couldn't predict was when. Other than obviously killing Papa Ezekiel himself, I am the only way out of this. I will not fight my fate; I was meant to die for my family. A willing sacrifice if it means that curse is broken and that baby be born without any burden. I only regret not being able to meet them and watch them grow, to watch my nephew be the family man he deserves to be."

He flinched as I approached, I stood in front of him watching him battle internally, he had been denied human touch for so long. So, I took his hands, placing them on my stomach. His eyes instantly fill with tears full of bottled-up emotion. "You hear my words. This is not YOUR fault; this was beyond your control. Your brother could have easily killed you and then we'd have no solution. He may have been under the control of evil, but I think a tiny sliver of him remained to make this possible. You are my child's great uncle, and I will always...always speak highly on how..." I choke back the sobs, "his uncle Gregory made our happiness possible. Thank you...for saving my Christian."

He shakes his head while I pull him into a hug. The years of torment burst through while he sobbed loudly. I can only imagine the self-torture he put himself through. After a few minutes, he steps back, "I'm sorry. I'm sorry for all of this. Can I see him?"

I know my face said it all, "Gregory, I don't think…"

"He's my nephew. Please! I need to say goodbye."

Fitz steps forward, "I'm not sure how present he is, Tavi seems to be growing stronger."

"Then we don't have much time, the stronger he becomes the weaker Chris gets. If too weak he could take over permanently. Take me to him now! The ceremony needs to take place sooner than later. I need to see what I am up against."

I follow him toward the dungeon when he stops me, "My beautiful niece, please let me do this alone. I don't want you to see him like this."

I was about to object but Miss Ren took my hand, "Come child, I will need you to memorize a part of the protection spell for the ceremony, your witch must be ready to also carry and wield the child's Legacy power."

I forgot about that. Kam told me that the twins' powers coursed through her when she had to battle John Michael and Bridget. I could harness my little one's power to help fortify the protection spell. I concede and follow the coven.

I lay in the darkness of my mind trying to not exert a lot of energy. I cannot believe my father would do this. I'm fucking glad he's dead. If he wasn't, I'd kill that bastard myself!

You'd have never beaten your father; he was a born leader. Your birth was a mistake, he didn't hide you to protect you! He was ashamed of you!

Yeah? Well, the feeling's fucking mutual.

K: Hey, get message from mate. They got plan, can't give details but working with witch coven.

Let them come and fail! Then watch helplessly as I take over your life. Your precious mate and worthless child will be the first to die! I'll enjoy plunging a knife into her stomach to rid of both parasites!

Kas shakes his head, whispering:

K: Plan will work. Save energy.

He lies down as I think of my wife and child. The way he described their death like it was something he looked forward to, I'd rather die first and take that coward with me! No way I'm giving him the satisfaction. There are too many memories ahead to give up now. Birth, first word, first steps, all the way until this mighty pack is handed over to my son or daughter.

I hear the dungeon doors clang opening and assume they're making their rounds.

"Sweet Moon Goddess, what has my brother done to you?"

It sounds like Uncle Gregory?! What's he doing here?

Tavi rears up as far as he can. "Well, if it isn't the prodigal brother himself. He should have killed you when he had the chance. You're both weak and inferior. When I take over, I'm going to rip open your ribcage and pluck your organs out one by one!"

I noticed the Amber hue from my uncle's being, but it was a weak glow, probably from lack of use. My father practiced every chance he got, which is why his glow was so powerful. You almost had to look away. Gregory's eyes were the same hazel color as mine as he hovered from the ground.

"Weak! Even your Legacy blood is ashamed of you! Why are you here? You can't get rid of me!"

My uncle chuckles, "Tavi, is it? All that research you did with my brother or Ezekiel, and you didn't think to scrub the Legacy history records? This possession has happened before, twice. It's been defeated before and will again." He said it with an air of confidence.

I felt Tavi shaking his head in disbelief. I was shocked, myself.

"I came to speak to my nephew. Let him come forward now!"

"He's much too weak! Can barely shout his pathetic begging anymore. It's no more than a whisper. He can hear you just fine."

My uncle winces thinking about how powerless Tavi told him I was.

"I'm so sorry, Chris, I should have tried harder. You shouldn't have to suffer because of my brother's blind ignorance. I'm going to fix this...I love you, nephew; always remember that."

Somehow those words, though grim, comfort me. They're up to something, but I know if nothing works and he gets too close to being free, I'll have to sacrifice us all. But how?

This is insanity and craziness all wrapped into one. Miss Ren briefs me on my role and I sit in my room with Calliope to harness all my energy from my being into one centralized location. My elevated powers should strengthen the protection spell tenfold, giving Chris a better chance to come out unharmed. He will be scarred emotionally, though and I don't know how he'll react to losing his Legacy status. I couldn't imagine losing Calliope unless it was life-threatening and for him, it is.

We can't wait any longer, especially if Tavi is telling the truth about Chris being so weak. The ceremony must take place tonight.

It was around 6 p.m. when I was summoned to the front door. I didn't want to see anyone until the ceremony. My emotions were all over the place and lack of concentration could kill my husband. I was told it was important, so I came down and around the staircase to see King and Queen Remington. I was basically their other daughter and seeing them made me tear up again.

I bow as gracefully as I can. "What are you doing here?!" Queen Melody opens her arms and I run into them, colliding with the loving warmth of my bonus parents. I am such a complete fucking mess.

"Kam and Kayd couldn't be here for obvious reasons, so we're here to help."

"Melody and her white witch, Illaria, can help in conducting the ceremony. Where is this uncle of his?" I could hear the disdain in his voice, he was not a fan.

"Gregory is meditating in his room, he said he needed some time to accept his fate. He knows he said it, but he hadn't mentally acknowledged it. Now he is."

Melody places her hands in front of her. "It is the ultimate sacrifice; we will leave him be in the meantime. The ceremony will start at midnight, the second day after the new moon is the best time for spells and rituals such as these. We'll need all advantages for this to work. Don't cry, my daughter. We will get him back."

"I hope so." Then I notice her smiling widely, "Never in a million years would I think my wild child would be settled down, married, and pregnant. Both you and Kam have made me a very proud grandmother." She rubs my stomach and her touch made me smile and made him move.

"Oh! He moved! I think he knew you were talking about him. It's his first kick!"

She pulls me in and I relish in it. I'm also gutted that Chris can't share this with me.

"Excuse me, King and Queen Remington." I hear Miss Ren's delicate voice behind me, I turn around to see her bow. "It's good to meet you in person." There's a powerful ambiance in her tiny demeanor. Malcolm extends his hand to kiss hers.

"And you as well, Miss Ren, but please, call us Malcolm and Melody."

"My husband is right. No need for formalities. We're here to provide additional support and energy to the ceremony. The Violet ceremony consisted of the five Elders and the sacrificial Legacy. How many do we have here?"

"My circle has four, five and a half with Vanessa, and the Legacy sacrifice but now with you adding to the power circle, the odds are slowly rising in our favor. He won't suspect outside help. He thinks we're a bunch of feeble old ladies."

Now I was curious, "Miss Ren, do you refer to yourselves as a bunch of witches? Because you're not a hybrid like me, but you learned witchcraft. What do you prefer to be called?"

She laughs at my curiosity. "We are a coven of a powerful combination of sorcery. We possess an emotional witch, a hedge witch, a ceremonial witch, and I am a hereditary witch, passed down from generation to generation by the women in my family. Combined, we can cure, heal, protect, defend, and a bevy of other requests. Nessa, being a silver moon witch, you harness a bit of the hereditary traits like me and that's why when I met you, I knew you would make an amazing Luna. Tonight, you will stretch beyond your boundaries, it will feel uncomfortable, but you must trust in your powers! That is the only rule you must remember, do not waver. It literally could mean life or death. Now, I'm not saying this to scare you, child. I have never lied or sugar-coated anything and I won't do it now. You will see our Alpha in excruciating pain. He may scream out in agony and plead for you to stop, but you have to see it through, or there may be a chance that the curse could be passed on to your little one."

"What?! Please tell me you're joking. To my son?! He's innocent in all this. Is there anything we can do to prevent any chance?"

I'm panicking. My entire being is shaking. Not my baby boy!

She grabs my shoulders and forces me to look in her eyes. "You must complete the ceremony in its entirety. There is no room for error, do you understand?" For fear of bawling, I nod my head.

Malcolm clears his throat, "Melody will need to prepare as well. Is there a room we can use?"

"Of course, please choose from one in that hallway and if you need anything, please let me or the staff know."

Melody follows her husband as they pick the first door on the left.

Miss Ren turns "Eat a hearty meal, then clean, and dress in all white. You represent the light in his life. I will get you when it's time. Remember all I taught you and all I told you. Have faith, darling."

I order a small meal, take a chapter from Gregory, and meditate until my food arrives. Trying to suppress those negative thoughts and replace them with all the precious moments we'll have.

I hope.

I lay motionless and hear Tavi chuckle as if he already won. I am weak but I've been exaggerating to get his guard down. I hate to admit it, but what he says is true. He is slowly taking my energy from me.

I meant what I said, I will sacrifice my life to save my wife and child. No husband would ever do anything else. Once committed, nothing is more important than the survival of your bloodline. Mine would continue in my child; they would rule this pack. My sacrifice a distant memory as they continue for generations to come.

She would never forgive me, though...breaking her heart and our bond, leaving her to fend for herself. She would cry hysterically as they lit the pyre with my body. She would curse my name but also beg for one more day in my arms. I pray to the Moon Goddess that it doesn't come to that.

I groan loudly and it echoes. Tavi continues to yank at the chains that bind him.

"Soon, I will be able to burn all these packs to the ground. Rule this world and bend it to my will!"

"And then what?"

He sputters; my response catches him off guard.

"After you complete my father's bidding, then what? He'll still be dead and you'll be another pawn under Papa Ezekiel's thumb. If anyone rules, it will be Papa Ezekiel; you're just his puppet. Do you even have your own thoughts? You have mine but do you ever think for yourself? You'll never be a whole entity. You never were. You were my father's lackey and soon, you'll be the yes man of a witch doctor. What makes you think he won't use you and use you until he no longer needs you? He's a powerful being who'll end you with a snap of his fingers. He won't save you! He'll discard you like the piece of trash you are! No one fell harder for my father's bullshit than you and for that, it will end badly and whether I die with you or not, you won't leave this dungeon alive and free, I promise you."

"Quite the dramatic speech, but I hold all the cards! Your promise means nothing! Your father empowered me to finish his great work, something you were too weak to do. I WAS THE SON HE WANTED! I made him proud!"

There it was the main reason to do my father's bidding. How pathetic...

"You're fucking delusional! Just like him, maybe you are his rightful son. You won't win...I won't let you." And with that, I lay silent as I waited for the signal from them. Kas was resting the entire time, I couldn't tell if he was in a trance or sleeping, but he did not perk up to our interaction. I was literally arguing with myself.

"Maybe you should do like the mutt, be a good boy, and play dead!"

I ignored him then I felt something in the pit of my stomach. It was a gentle warmth that seemed to comfort me. Then, a whisper in my ear.

Prepare and listen for instruction. I love you, my Alpha King.

I knew her voice anywhere, they were preparing for battle.

We told the pack about the ceremony and that they should steer clear of the dungeon area. "Yes, Luna." they all chimed. I had a few individuals offer extra power if we needed a boost. Miss Ren thanked them and told them she would summon them if needed. They would all be outside in the training area awaiting orders. There were no hybrids like me, but a lot of them practiced spells, incantations, alchemy, and rites.

I had eaten and dressed in a simple off-the-shoulder dress. My hair fell on both sides with loose curls.

N: Calliope, be honest, can we do this?

I ask because I am worried, worried I may lose my husband.

C: Absolutely, I will harness power from the tiny hybrid and Dalila will protect you and shift if need to. I can feel the exponential power of this child, it is more than enough.

D: Relay message to Kas to get ready. He said husband had spat with stupid witch then silent. He might be too weak or playing dead.

When she said dead, my heart dropped. I know she said playing but still. I clutched my chest to stop myself from hyperventilating.

D: Sorry. Husband okay, Kas tell me just now. Dalila sorry.

N: It's okay, I'm so nervous! I need Chris, it's not just me anymore. We have a son to raise and hand over the pack to, I need him here for all the milestones. I can't do this without him. I..."

There's a knock and Fitz walks in. He'll be standing by as security, so he's dressed in all black... like Chris does. Everything reminds me of him.

The days of ruling have taken a toll on him. He was obviously exhausted but more worried that his best friend was in trouble and he couldn't help. He stood there for a moment, observing me. I know he's trying to be strong for me.

"Fitz, come here." He sits on the cedar chest in front of our bed.

"Chris would be so proud at how you easily took over the pack. When he chose you, he knew his brother could deliver and you did. I know you're tired; maybe you should sit this out. He'd kill me if something happened to you."

"And I'd die if I wasn't there to help in some way. I'll sleep when I'm dead and that's that, Nessa. I'm right there beside you to save my best friend."

I don't argue, they have a bond so strong, they felt each other's pain and witnessed great milestones in each other's lives. I couldn't wait to see them together again.

"Okay, let's go save our Alpha."

Everyone is waiting downstairs, the coven dressed in an array of colors that signify their witch with protective marks on their arms. The Remington's dressed in black and white to recognize her white witch, which reminded me to ask:

"If Tavi sees them, won't he blow a fuse? Will it make it worse, could he retaliate?"

"I will bring her in at the precise moment the power is needed and not a moment sooner. We will have the element of surprise. Everyone gathers so the coven can cast a protection barrier around you, slightly different than a spell; it refracts whatever he may try to throw at you. He will try to lash out in any way that he can to stay in control of Alpha Christian."

The four ladies cover us, holding up their hands, "Oh Moon Goddess, we call upon you to protect our divine coven against this evil entity that plagues our Alpha.

Give us the power to remove him with minimum harm. Protect those here who fight alongside us. Refract any negativity the being may use to harm or distract us. We seek you as divine power. We humble ourselves and ask for your mercy."

I felt a warmth embodying me, but we weren't in any sunlight or overhead lightning; it was the dead of night. I open my eyes to see Miss Ren smiling, "Now we are protected by the Moon Goddess herself. Are we ready?"

Was I ready? Ready to face the evil cohabitating within my husband? He was so cold and vicious. His words toward me and my child hurt. Chris would never say those vile disgusting things, but... what if we're too late?

I am brought out by two hands squeezing my shoulders and for a moment I see my love, then blink to see it was Gregory holding me.

I sighed disappointingly, "Christian..." He pulls me in and kisses my forehead. "Don't give up before we start. Don't...don't let my death be in vain. Do you hear me?! My nephew and his son deserve a life together, now let's go."

That crushed me, the words of a dying man, a sacrificial lamb. I would make sure his bravery would be told for ages to come. He steps back, holds out his hand, and I put mine in his as we trek towards the dungeon. When I looked toward it the Remington's were standing slightly away from the coven who were chanting. The ground below them was marked in these white symbols that would glow and fade. The glow got so intense that I had to look away.

And then I heard Chris screeching from inside. I didn't hesitate, I ran toward the door and pulled it open.

I try to get through quickly. I had yet to master teleportation like the Remington's. No matter, I pushed myself forward as fast as I could, but as I burst through his screams were replaced with laughter, evil, vindictive laughter.

"Ahahahaha, you fool! Seeing the hurt and disappointment on your face brings me such delight. Are you ready to say goodbye to your weakling of a mate? If I were a sick sadistic bastard, I'd end you and that wretched child. Who knows, I still might…" He smirked and for the first time, I did not see Christian but the evil that overpowered him. I don't know how I could separate them, but I could. It was like he was glitching and I saw the evil that befell my husband. His soul was black, heartless. His eyes were red like fire and his hair was short and shaggy not like Chris' beautiful locs that flowed over his shoulders.

That was enough for Calliope to roar forward and for once I did not stop her; in fact, I stepped aside. She knew not to physically hurt him, but her presence is overpowering. It was a statement, an exclamation point not to misunderstand.

DON'T FUCK WITH MY FAMILY!

The wind whipped around the enclosed place as he shielded his eyes until it died down.

"I have warned you it is detrimental if you continue your anger towards my baby. Your time is over, and I am here to rid Christian of this diseased part of him, you cancerous leech! He doesn't need you to be a great Alpha, you need him to feel like more than what you are… a component, a part, a piece of equipment only used when needed. You aren't even a man. I can see your true form and you don't scare me!"

My ears tuned in to the chanting from outside, then they switched their chant, and I could see it heavily irritated him as their quiet chants became loud and boisterous.

"Curse those wretched old hags! I'll shut them up!"

Everything happened so fast, I saw him raise his arms as far as he could, then quickly thrust them down and a white cloud burst from underneath him. The force was so strong as it acted like a shockwave, roaring past me and through the thick stone and metal of the building, knocking me off balance, but Calliope landed upright safely, protecting me and the baby. I realized the chanting had stopped from above.

"Ahh, peace and quiet! Now I can focus. *Malahik nevim poster abi…* I call my master to grant me the ability to separate from my host and take over!"

"No!" I heard myself scream internally as Calliope shot her hands up and sent a shock wave back knocking him off his knees, lying him flat on the ground.

I feel that lump in my throat as I try to choke it down. "Please don't do this, don't make me fight you." Never in a million years would I think I'd have to use my magic on my own husband.

He rears up to that position to knock me off my feet again, but this time, I conjure a magic rope to bind him, wrapping him tightly; he coughs and then gasps.

"What…what's going on? Nes, why am I down here? I don't understand why you're doing this?" I felt the emotions of the whole fiasco drain down my face. I'm broken, and my only saving grace is the one who's hurting me. Or is it me who's hurting him? He looks so confused about why he was here.

Which was a dead giveaway.

"This was Chris's choice, he warned us, you liar!" I tightened the grip, and he growled, revealing what I already knew. It was a ploy and I saw evil once again.

"I'll kill you! You'll regret crossing me when I rip that fetus from your womb and crush it, slamming its lifeless body on the ground."

Moon goddess...he's a monster! I tried to reason with Calliope, but she was conjuring a fireball in her right hand while holding the ropes. I immediately felt the helplessness Chris did when he lost control.

N: Calliope, no! STOP! Miss Ren, it's now or never!

The Coven comes in, chanting and circling him. He laughs at their attempt." I knew I should have killed you. Your incessant chanting won't change anything!"

He starts his own chanting while bolts of light shoot from his hands toward the coven, but it bounces off their protection, which further angers him. I see Fitz behind them, trying not to let his anger control his shifting.

Little did he know their chanting was to give Christian the strength to separate without irreversible damage.

I hope we're doing this right.

That monster put her in danger! Then he threatened to murder my child! I'm not sure who's in control or if they're working together, but they could land safely after Tavi blew her off her feet. She retaliated naturally and knocked him on our ass, he deserved it. Calliope is seconds away from torching me for the despicable things he said. Then so be it. I was never meant for happiness. I was doomed the moment I was born a Legacy, the moment my father thought he found another way to see his plan through. I wish I was never born.

I can hear the chanting and I see Miss Ren and her Coven around again like last time except... except I can feel a soothing warmth surrounding me. The longer they chant, the stronger I feel, like a phone on a fast charge.

He's so worried about getting rid of them, he's not even paying attention to how this is affecting me. Kas is now standing taller and more confident as he reveals his sharp canines, his fur standing up and he's in a combative stance.

K: Kas feel great energy. Feel invincible but mate says wait for cue.

Dalila must be able to relay messages while Nessa is deep in the chanting. I remember reading that the mother of a Legacy child can harness their energy if they need to. She and my child are involved. I never felt prouder and terrified.

I watched and felt Tavi twist and contort my body in dangerous angles like he was trying to physically break me and cause me permanent damage.

He lets out a bellow of a growl, "Whatever your weak little plan is isn't going to work! Once I summon my Master, he will help me end your pathetic mate." Tavi closes his eyes and now I'm in a state of unknown though I can still hear them.

"I call upon my Master to fulfill my wish I was promised in exchange for my obedience! Let me permanently take my place as head of this body, to cast the other entities to the depths of Hell. *Allum shava pren....*"

As he continues his chant or prayer, I see a silhouette forming on the other side of the darkness in my mind. Kas was growling and ready to pounce as it took shape and it looked like, "Uncle Gregory? How are you doing this?"

He smiled, "There's so much I want to say to you, my only nephew. I pray for your peace after this ordeal and know that I will be watching over you, protecting you from the great beyond. It is my eternal duty I happily take."

I was so confused like he was speaking in code, "The great beyond? But you're not…" Then it hit me, why he was here, why he told me he would fix things, why he didn't seem weak and afraid anymore. No, he looked healthy, his glow strong and undoubtedly powerful in his being. He also looked much younger and refreshed, like the man I remember years ago.

"What are you going to do?"

"What I have to do. What has been my purpose all along. I was so relieved to see you step out of the SUV that day, I didn't trust Tomas to bring you back alive."

"He killed grandma! He came to me in a dream, or nightmare, and told me he should have killed me, too. I knew something was wrong when she didn't look out the window to wave goodbye. I regret leaving her with that monster! She knew and she didn't warn me so I could protect her. She knew…" I croaked out in a sob, reliving our final moment and all the ways I could have saved her.

"This was not your fault, if he hadn't done it, then he would have done it eventually. Papa Ezekiel saw her gift as dangerous once she predicted his very explicit death. If he got rid of her maybe he could prevent it. I assume he's hiding away surrounded by protection to avoid it, hence why he has not made an appearance." That would make sense. He has shown no signs of answering Tavi. I bask in his failure. Gregory steps forward, "Don't blame yourself, I know she's up there proud of the man you have become, I know I am. Live by your rules, love as you've never been loved before, be better than my brother. That niece of mine is a firecracker and in the brief time, I can see how good she is for you. You tell her every day... how much you love her." He looks away trying to will the tears not to fall and he clears his throat. "It's time to rectify my part in all this. Take care, Chris and remember...I do this for you."

And before I could ask what he would do he disappeared. I got that feeling in the pit of my stomach. I already knew the answer, like with my grandmother. Haven't I lost enough?! I will literally have no family left except the one I created. Now I need to shake the notion of dying and get back.

I hear Tavi shriek as I look from the inside out. Everyone's still chanting. I feel the best I've felt in days, better than my normal strength, if not more.

"I see you've given him his strength back, but I am much stronger, he doesn't stand a chance against the power of Papa Ezekiel!"

He throws up his hands like he's waiting to receive something. Nothing happens. He tries once more, "Curses! Why won't you give me what I'm owed?! I've done everything you asked of me, I was the son you wanted, the one man enough to carry out your purpose. WHAT MORE DO YOU WANT?!" He growls out and that's when Uncle Gregory steps into the dungeon, his bare chest marked with symbols every Legacy recognizes, the mark of sacrificial death.

Each Legacy should take it upon themselves to learn the history, good and bad, of the Legacy dynasties and I was aware of the past two breaches to the Legacy line, I never thought I'd be the third. I remember Tavi's surprised reaction to hearing this has happened before. He must have been away plotting my demise when I was discovering about them.

Tavi glared at Gregory, "You try to perform the ritual on me?! You're much too weak a Legacy for it to work."

"Says the lackey who got no answer from their Master. Where is he now, huh? My brother doesn't acknowledge you, you're a failure! He tossed you aside and now it's time to finally rid us of you. Miss Ren, now!"

She breaks from the circle and Nessa takes her place at the head while Miss Ren recites something in Latin that makes Gregory's Legacy glow bright as the Sun. Tavi shields his face as much as he can all chained up, but this display only angered him as he screams out his frustration causing a wind tunnel in the small space, but the ladies did not waiver.

"Nessa, cupcake, it's me, Christian. Don't let them do this to me, they're going to kill me. Nessa, I love you. Help me." He's on his knees pleading to her and I can see her lip quivering, she desperately wanted to believe wholeheartedly that it was me. I could not believe he was trying to get her to stop what she was doing. He knew she wielded plenty of power. I pound against the wall. "You scumbag!"

Then she surprises me by sending a bolt of lightning that hits us in the chest. I didn't feel the effect but felt it knock us off our feet, but the chains slam us back down.

"Nice try, Tavi but Chris would never call me cupcake." She raised her dropped hand up and chanted harder and louder. Releasing her anger and frustration of it all. I know she's exhausted and heartbroken.

"Well, cupcake, I thought I'd give it a try." He laughs hysterically and I see her wince, wanting to cry, but she refocused.

I notice movement and see Gregory pull a butterfly knife and traced the markings on his chest, but he does not bleed. "I sacrifice myself and my Legacy blood in the name of the Moon Goddess to liberate my nephew, Alpha Christian Evan Grey, and the Midnight Shadow pack from this internal evil. I sacrifice all my power and life force to drag the damned to the depths of Hell and I will rise to the great beyond after my task is completed. *Vinictum Iserip Tavanimum*...I sacrifice my life and my Legacy!" The wounds glow, Amber, as I feel the pull towards the outside, but I wait for my cue. The wind picks up as he continues to chant,

"I SACRIFICE MY LIFE, MY LEGACY FOR MY NEPHEW, MOON GODDESS RID US OF THIS DARK ENTITY AND GIVE HIM HIS LIFE BACK UNHARMED!"

Tavi laughs, "You don't wield enough power! You need more and your brother is dead. No one is here to help you!" He laughs but then clutches his neck as if he were choking. He was struggling to breathe, and I was slowly being pulled to the forefront of my mind.

"NO! Where is that power coming from?! It's...stronger than mine! It... can't be!"

Then I saw the Violet glow from the crack of the door before the Queen of the Violet Legacies stepped forward in all her Legacy glory. I know she had a special mother-daughter bond with Nessa and she traveled here to help.

"You bring the enemy onto my grounds?! A woman no less. She can't be the source of power; no woman would hold that power properly! Where is your husband, why would he send his meek wife in alone? The coward!" He hisses, but the Queen remains stoic. She lifts her hand and touches Gregory's shoulder creating an orange-like hue between them and they both turn toward Tavi. "You underestimate the power of women, you pathetic entity! We bear children, raise families, keep our packs in order, wielding tremendous power without going mad. We appreciate our gift; we hone that gift and never use it in any other way than the Moon Goddess intends it. You try to insult me as a female Violet Legacy when the truth is I will ALWAYS be more powerful than you!"

Her response was so classy and yet filled with the venom he needed to hear. I understand why Nessa loved her so much. Even with the combined glow, her amethyst eyes were mesmerizing as I watched them.

Their combined power caused him to scream out as if he were in pain, yet I didn't feel it. I felt I was right behind him and that I could remove him from control at the perfect moment.

"I combine my Violet Legacy with my Amber Legacy brother in his quest to vanquish the evil within his nephew. Moon Goddess, grant him peace and a safe journey home to you as he makes the ultimate sacrifice. Brother Gregory, finish reciting there isn't much time!"

I see the Coven has gone from raising their arms high to aiming them at us. Tavi seems unable to move his arms as he was trying to so he could hurl things and cause distraction, but they were firmly at his side as he screamed out, "No! This isn't supposed to happen! NO!"

The chanting changes once more and I feel as if I am floating above him, but it also feels like I am being ripped in half. It was a dull, irritating pain but only on my right side, where Tavi usually hung out. Kas is floating next to me, and his ears are down as he can also feel that pain.

"I know, Kas. Just a little bit longer."

What I am witnessing is something I will never forget. The raw power in this room is exponential, but Tavi is refusing to give up without a fight we must complete this before Papa Ezekiel decides to come and grant his wish. We don't know how powerful he is; powerful enough to cause members to turn against their own.

"Nessa, coven, the protection of the separation spell now!" Miss Ren yells as she takes her place next to me again.

"*Protectum solum divinium.* Protect our Alpha as we cast out the impurity! Protect our Alpha's physical and mental being! Return him as he once was before he was deceived!"

We continue the chant as Melody and Gregory continue to glow with this combination of Amber and Violet. It's beautiful visually but also deadly.

Melody acknowledges Gregory, giving the go ahead. Gregory pulls the blade again, holding it high above his head. "I sacrifice my Legacy to return this hostile Legacy energy to the depths of darkness. May he flourish without him!" Then he looks Tavi dead in the eyes. "I take the evil Tavarious with me in death and condemn him to Hell where he belongs!" Then he rams the blade into his abdomen. "OOF!" He and Tavi shriek, but for Tavi, it was as if he was on fire. His glow was flickering and sputtering like it was going out.

"NOOOOO! Papa Ezekiel will find a way! He always finds a way and he'll bring me back!" Chris collapsed and stopped moving, he is positioned the same as Gregory's lifeless body and it scares me. I stopped chanting and was about to run to him to see if he was okay. "Nessa, keep chanting! It's not over yet. We must finish!"

My heart needs to know he's okay.

Please don't be dead, please. My heart is screaming to run to him. Dalila is whimpering and walking in circles, trying to sense Kas. Calliope is standing and waiting for any sign of movement. I feel like time has stopped, or I stopped breathing, I couldn't tell.

"Moon Goddess, grant us our will! We thank you and honor you for giving us our powers and using them to save our Alpha. We ask for a sign..." Then the entire room got deathly quiet, I was looking for dust to know he was breathing, but I wasn't seeing any. I feared the worst until, "Ooh! He kicked me; our son kicked me!"

Miss Ren places her hand on my stomach and closes her eyes before smiling. "Strong like his father. I consider that a great sign. We need to make sure it is our Alpha before we unchain him. Someone call the pack doctor."

I cautiously kneel next to his limp body, and I push him to his back, mindful of the shackles. He looks like he's been through war, and he has, mentally and physically. It's been so draining. I may have had the help of our son, but I was feeling fatigued myself. I brush the dirt off his face where he collapsed.

"My Alpha King... please, we need you. Me and...your son. We're going to have a boy, isn't that wonderful? I know you'd be proud if we had a boy or a girl. You were thankful we started our family. Your family needs you! I need you..." I squeak out through the tears before I hear the doctor enter.

Melody places her hands on my arms to pull me away so the doctor could check on him. I felt it all hit me and I turned around and she held me while I cried my eyes out.

"Sshhh, my darling daughter, you must stay strong for your husband. It is the wife who keeps the man together. They are nothing without their mates." I see her concern for me and I try to pull myself together. "He needs to be in the hospital. We can chain him to the bed, but he needs medical attention and tests now."

Fitz calls the twins in after I call for them to unchain and take him to the pack hospital. They look me over before they unchain him and I smile. They treat me like family, like their sister, and I am thankful.

"I'm okay, we're okay, I promise. Just make sure to get him the care he needs."

They unchain him and carry him out. It was so much that I didn't realize I was swaying and everything went black before I could say anything.

The pain was mind-numbing as we separated from Tavi. At the moment Gregory sacrificed himself by plunging the blade, Kas roared forward, clamp on his arm and drag Tavi out of control, giving me the ability to regain power.

Then as Kas was yanking him down to the ground, Gregory appeared. He wrapped his arms around Tavi's, recited something and then there was a bright glow and Tavi's wailing before they were both gone. And all was quiet as Kas came to me panting.

K: Evil witch gone but so is uncle. He save us both.

C: Yeah, he saved our lives. I'll never forget and I'll make sure it's written in our history book.

Then I felt a rush of heat before the world spun.

C: I don't feel so good, what...what about you?

K: Kas sleepy...very...

Then he collapses and before I knew it, everything went black.

"Nessa...Nessa, honey, wake up!"

Ugh, what happened?! I feel like I got hit by a Mack truck. My energy level was 10% and I was being generous. It was exhausting to open my eyes, but I saw everyone staring at me worriedly. The Remington's, Miss Ren, Fitz, and the twins. I'm in my bed, but I recognize they are all dressed differently. I hold my head and sigh, "How long have I been out?"

"You said you were fine before we hauled Chris to the hospital." Fitz was upset and rightly so, but I didn't have an answer; it all happened so fast. I thought I was okay.

Melody smiles at me, "It's been a day, my child. You exerted a massive amount of energy. Your body shut down and just because you are awake now doesn't mean you are ready. You are on mandatory bed rest for at least a week. Doctor's and mom's orders! Don't you dare think to argue with me, either. Miss Ren mirrors my sentiment, and she will update me on your progress until you have that baby. Do you understand?"

Not a side I usually see from them, the stern parents, but I was not crazy to talk back. I agree and she kisses my forehead and squeezes my hand. "We are so very proud of you. We're headed home. We'll check on you tomorrow."

"Thank you for your help, I really mean it. You saved my husband."

Malcolm leans down to kiss my forehead, "We only helped. His uncle sacrificed his life. Never forget what Gregory did for this pack. Take care, dear."

Once they leave, I look at everyone else, "Where is Chris? Is he…?" Everyone rushes forward to sit somewhere on my bed and Fitz laughs, I fail to see the humor.

"He's fine. He's being monitored to see what kind of damage he took from the separation. The Amber elders are with him now to make sure that no part of Tavi remains. He should be good soon and only then will we know the extent. You know, the whole pack is celebrating his return. As soon as you two are well enough, we will host a picnic. Get some rest, I still have a pack to run. Come on, guys, let's wrap up as much as we can so Chris doesn't have to deal with anything in the foreseeable future.

Miss Ren is the last one remaining. "Miss Ren, tell me the truth, is he going to be okay?"

"Oh yes, child, we fortified him before the separation. We were blessed to have Queen Melody's assistance. She and that baby were the boosts we needed to push us forward. Now he rests to get his strength back. He may not immediately realize he's missing his Legacy power, but he may take it hard when he does. He may feel remorse and regret. You need to be there to tell him he's still a great and powerful man. Get some rest and we'll update you on his status later."

My mind was racing with possibilities, the good and the bad, I got my husband back but not at 100%. How will this affect his personality?

I don't want to lay in my empty bed, I want to be the first thing he sees when his eyes open. I slip on my robe and against my guard's orders, I make my way to the infirmary.

"Luna, you're supposed to be resting, please. Alpha Christian will have a fit if anything happens to you." The doctor looks worried about his own well-being. Chris has a temper, but that is a hot-blooded male trait all Alphas possess, even Kayd. He is the sweetest guy in the world, but if you threaten Kam or his family, you will see a monster. I heard how he ripped his so-called "brother" John Michael apart after he tried to claim the throne and take Kam away from him.

I turned to the doctor, "I understand, Doctor Taylor, I wanted to rest with my husband. Is that possible to accommodate? I assure you I will not let the Alpha harm you in any way, I will take full responsibility."

"Yes, ma'am. Let us pull out the adjustable bed to make it wide enough for you to fit comfortably. He's been in a dream-like state with mumbling, but we can't make out what he is saying. He's still very weak and we need to see what the damage is once he becomes conscious. Perhaps the touch of his mate will bring him out of this state."

"Perhaps... thank you, Doctor Taylor." I sit down and look around. A few nurses are keeping their eye on me, I must look a sight in my gown and robe sporting a beach ball for a belly. Ok, it might not be that big, but Legacy pregnancies are much faster in development and shorter. Kam's was six months instead of nine; not sure, though. I know my time is condensed with my magical kid here. I pat my stomach, "Thank you, my sweet boy, for helping save your daddy's life. Already taking the steps into your rightful place as heir to the Midnight Shadow pack. I pray you never have to go through anything your father and I did. I can't wait to meet you."

"Luna, the bed is ready, and we moved some of the medical equipment around so it should not interfere."

Fitz: Nessa, where are you? You're supposed to be on...

Nessa: Bed rest...blah blah blah, I know. I am resting with my husband. Good night Fitz: you've also had a long day. I'll see you in the morning.

Fitz: Just as hard-headed as he is...

Nessa: What?!

Fitz: Nothing, goodnight, Luna

After a couple of rocks, I used the momentum to end up on my feet. A nurse leads the way with a blanket and pillow in her hand.

I guess the beeping is a good sign then I notice he's handcuffed to the bed. "What?"

"The acting Alpha ordered it until he woke up. I'm sorry, ma'am."

"No, it's not your fault and he's right; it's a bit overwhelming on the heartstrings. I'll take the blanket; I don't need the pillow. Set it in the chair." She bows and lays the pillow in the chair before leaving us alone.

He's lying on his back, and his chest is rising and falling, which matches the blips on the monitor. I lean forward and graze my hand against his cheek. "Chris, I'm here. I'm not leaving you until you wake up, do you hear me?" I lean back until I fall against him and I open the blanket to cover us. I slide under his non-handcuffed arm with my belly resting on him. I wrap my arm around his waist. Then I gaze up at his face, so calm and carefree.

"Hey, I'm here. Kas if you can hear me, we're all here, me, Calliope, Dalila, and our son. We need you two to get better. I'll be here every day until you come back to me."

I don't know when I fell asleep, but I remember reliving the events from earlier but with such a grim outcome, much different from what happened. I shot up, gasping for air, and it took a moment to gather my surroundings and remember what happened. I glanced at the window to see the sun was rising, so it was around 7 a.m. I look over and am shocked to see him staring at me.

"Chris?"

"Is this a dream? Don't wake me if it is, I really want to be with her. Don't take her away from me, please. She's been through too much already without me." He's pleading as if this were a dream and I'd disappear at any moment. I smile, then lean forward to kiss him and his strong arm automatically wraps around me. I lean back and see his smile a mile wide. "This is no dream, sweetheart. I'm here with you. I needed to make sure you were okay. Dalila and Calliope were worried."

"I thought she didn't do human emotion?"

Calliope: I made an exception. It won't happen again.

And she shuffles back into the depths as I laugh at her.

"What happened, what she witnessed, what she felt changed her. Oh, and the tiny human, as she calls them."

He blinks as if he just remembered I was pregnant and his hands shot over to caress my stomach.

"You really are showing now. You're so beautiful carrying my child, Nes. Everything happened so fast! From me finding out, to finding Gregory, to Tavi taking over. I said so many hurtful things, I didn't mean any of it. I'm sorry!"

He shakes his head and I shush him while grabbing his hand. "It wasn't you; it was never you. You would never speak so ill of the people who love you, we know that. Focus on your healing, not the past."

He sighs hard and his brow furrows when his handcuff rattles and catches his attention. He looked to me for an answer. "It's uh...we didn't know for sure if he was gone and we couldn't risk it. I can call him to come to unlock you now, the Amber Legacy elders came to confirm."

"It's uh...we didn't know for sure if he was gone and we couldn't risk it. I can call him to come to unlock you now, the Amber Legacy elders came to confirm."

I pull her close to kiss her forehead. "No, I'm sure Fitz is exhausted. I can handle a few more hours being chained up. He was right to make that decision." I kiss her again as she holds on tighter. "I'm glad my beautiful wife was here when I opened my eyes. Kas is still sleeping, but I'm sure he'll be so excited to talk to Dalila again."

"She is more than excited, but she is lying in wait. But...how do you feel? Do you feel complete or like a part of you is missing? Do you remember everything?"

"Every excruciating detail. It will haunt me for the rest of my life. Nothing more than my hatred for my father and everything he put me through and threatened my child with the curse. He is responsible for the death of my mother, my grandmother, and now my uncle. He took everything from me!"

I felt my anger surge, but her momentary fear extinguished all the hate I was feeling. "Sorry. Let's lie here, I don't want to rile my baby up unnecessarily." I rub her belly.

"Your son."

"What?"

"You're going to have a son, Christian. Oh! Here, feel him?! He's been so active since the battle. Can you feel him kick?"

Could I?! It was single-handedly the most beautiful thing on Earth. Through all the pain and turmoil, this moment makes it worth it. I watch the impressions form and then disappear from her stomach. I even had a brief touching moment between father and son.

"My Goddess. What did I do to deserve this beautiful moment?"

"You fought. Plain and simple. You fought long and you fought hard to make it back to me and our little one. We have so much to do now, we have to build the nursery onto or in the suite and we need a car."

"I have an entire garage."

"Of high-end export cars, none of them fit or are safe for a baby, and I am not driving them, period." I kiss her forehead, "Yes, my love. I'll have it ready for you in a few days or whenever they clear me."

"Do you feel the same or different without your sorcerer? I know it's weird to ask, but do you want to talk to a mental health professional? I mean, seriously, you lost a big part of yourself and it's going to take time to cope, but to also realize that you're still a tough, badass Alpha."

I hear her and I know what she means. She's right, I feel different, I don't feel like myself, and I don't feel whole. It's all so much in such a little time. Kas is still reeling from the effects, he has been lying on his side since we blacked out. He assured me he was okay, just that he needed to gain his strength. I've never seen him so worn down. But I'm thankful for his effort in all this. I didn't need another part of me besides Kas, he's been my number one since the beginning. The sorcerer part of me was like my father, sneaky and ruthless, not looking out for my best interest. Does that make me feel like half a man or inadequate? I'd be lying if I said I didn't feel a little different, but I will recoup what I lost. I'm coming back better, stronger.

"I will talk to someone eventually, promise. But for now, we rest. I think it's safe to say we can sleep in today. Fitz can run the pack for a bit longer." She takes my hand and places it on her stomach and I spend a moment feeling the ripples and movement of my little one, my son.

My son.

I have no idea how much time has passed, but I see my entire leadership staring back at me. Nessa is still asleep, but they uncuffed me and we walked out to the hallway.

"How are you feeling, boss?" Kellan asks me as they surround me. I kept rubbing my wrist where it was cuffed because it hadn't healed 100%.

"I'm okay; no signs of him being around, but it seriously wore Kas out and it'll take some time before he and I are fully recharged. I want to run the pack a bit differently, I don't want to rank you because you all did well while I was indisposed. I want to run this as a partnership. We keep the titles but know that each of you is equally as qualified to run our pack. But don't let it go to your head...Fitz!"

He looked shocked that I called him out. "No, you need to worry about the Barbie twins over there! Who was the one who bagged a girl under the guise of being an Alpha?! Yeah..." It feels good to hear them laugh and joke, it feels good to be. I watched a small figure approach and knew it was Miss Ren.

"Good morning, Alpha. You look well, let me just..." She runs her hands around my person with her eyes closed. "No sign of him. You are purged of that evil entity! Such a horrible thing was placed upon you by your father. Had I known, I would have bound him to prevent this from even starting. But you came out of this stronger, wiser, and more aware of what's important. Where is my favorite Luna, by the way?"

"She's in there asleep. She's been taking good care of me."

"That's what good Lunas do. I'm going to check on her."

For the next three days, I am monitored for signs of re-emergence or anything that shouldn't be there. The coven has placed a protection spell around me and the entire pack grounds.

I hadn't forgotten my situation with Damian; news of this would send him into overdrive. This was business between us, the Cheshires, and the Violet Legacies. A bond forged not out of only necessity but out of respect. I respect them even more after the ordeal.

When I return to my office, I am surprised by the lack of work left on my desk, it looks like my crew handled any and everything. I look out my window and see the kids running around, security running training drills and...what is she doing?!

I see Nessa, rather Calliope, out in the combat area. I never moved so fast in my life; even Kas perked up, wondering what our mate was doing in her condition.

C: If he sees you practicing, he'll be out here immediately.

N: Pregnant or not, I need to stay combat ready. You saw what happened to him! I wouldn't have been much help if I didn't have my baby's power. I need to know as much as I can from Miss Ren and her coven, so next time...I'm not so helpless.

C: Mate coming. He is not happy.

"Vanessa Ann Vanderbilt-Grey, have you completely lost your mind?!"

"Watch yourself, Mr. Grey. We are not happy with your approach. I know what you're going to say and I am fine, honest. I don't want to be caught off guard like that again. I will be an amazing Luna and an even superior warrior! I don't want to argue about this because I put my foot down and that's final, do you understand?"

By the time she was done, her hair had fallen from her beautiful red curls to that metallic hue, and I knew Calliope had made her presence to stamp it in stone. I hold my hands up and back away with a simple, "Yes, dear." I may be the Alpha, but she is the boss of me.

I spent the next two weeks in therapy sessions because this was some heavy shit. I lost a part of me; a persona and I was dealing with the lies and betrayal.

"Tell me, Alpha. What would you describe as your most painful revelation in this ordeal?"

I'm lying on the stereotypical brown leather couch while Dr. Bennett tries to analyze me. Everyone insists that I do this and that it doesn't make me any less of a leader. Says those who are not seated here.

"The most painful revelation? There isn't just one. The fact that my father sold my sorcerer like he sold his soul. Or the fact that my uncle knew but didn't tell me? Or how about the fact that my mother and grandmother were innocent bystanders? I lost my entire family because of my father! THAT is the painful revelation. I wish I weren't his seed and I fear that my son might be affected. I live in fear every day until his birth and will every day after the fact because, like me, he is innocent. I fought hard to ensure he didn't live as I did. I will forego the Legacy tradition of hiding him away because it does more harm than good. I will be the one to tell him he's special and help him learn his powers even if I no longer have mine. My son...will not suffer...from my mistakes, ever!"

I'm panting and my hands are gripped tightly as all the emotions roll forward. I close my eyes and calm my breathing.

"Yes, Alpha, breathe it out. It's natural to harbor these feelings, but you must not hold on to them. That is what these sessions are for, for you to safely express all those pent-up emotions that you try not to show to appear weak. You've been progressing ahead of my schedule. Take that information and be proud of yourself." He gazes at his watch, "And your hour is up. See you this time next week, sir."

I feel better, but I'm smiling, knowing what is coming next. It's tradition after each session, a soak in the jacuzzi with my mate. She treats me to a shoulder and neck massage while I rub her tired and sore feet. She continues her Luna duties and field training as if she's not about to give birth. She is, due to my previous Legacy status, her pregnancy is between 5-7 months.

I climb the stairs three at a time, reaching our doors quickly. "Nes…" I open the door to hear water running in the bathtub. I made my way to the bathroom door to see her slipping off her robe, which sparked both my and Kas' senses. She looks over her shoulder with that smirk that makes me want to punish her.

"Well, hello, Mr. Grey, I thought I was going to have to start without you." I peel off my clothes slowly as her eyes widen and she licks her lips, "I wouldn't recommend that, Mrs. Grey, unless you want to be punished. I'm beginning to think that is exactly what you want, isn't it?"

She slides back against the furthest wall placing her arms up on the lip of the tub. She used a bath bomb and the bubbles are blocking my view. I growl as I approach my prey until I feel like I'm being set on fire as I step in.

"Is this comfortable for you?! It's like lava!"

"It's a bit cool but I can tolerate it."

I suppose her red hair and fiery disposition correlate to the freakishly hot water I am now steeping in. I carefully lower myself because I would like to have full use of my manhood.

"Ah! Sh... OH! Oh, oh...this is much hotter than last time. This may be our only kid at this point!" That gets a laugh from her. I finally got situated, her hands connected to my shoulders, and I can feel the tension disappearing.

"Thank you, sunflower."

"No problem. How did this session go?"

"It was fucking intense when he asked me what my most painful revelation was about all this happening. The trauma, expressing my rage in a healthy manner, etcetera, etcetera. You know, as much as I hate to admit this, it will probably torture me for the rest of my life, but if it ends with me, I can live with that burden. He only needs to focus on being the best Alpha after his father."

"And he will be. We don't know the outcome of all this besides I have you back in my arms and we are growing our family. We can only take it one day at a time, and I want you to know, Christian, I will be there to hold your hand every step of the way. I love you, my bad boy biker Alpha."

"You too, my fiery Queen. And now, time for you to relax. I know how swollen your feet get being on them all day. Knowing you'd go against doctor's and husband's orders to relax."

"Maybe I like the special treatment I'm getting." The water splashes from her raising and lowering her arms.

"I'm sure. We'll order dinner in bed and then it's off to sleep for you two.

Hours later:

I visit my parent's graves. I turn toward my mother's plot. "I'm so sorry you had to die because of him. We were supposed to have more time, but he took that away from me! If I could, I'd remove him from here and bury him in a landfill where he belongs. Not with you or Nana." I lean over, kiss her plot, and lean further to kiss my grandmother's.

Chris...Christian...

"Mom?" I look up and there is my mother, adorned in white. She still looked as beautiful as she was when she was alive. Although beautiful, the look on her face was concerning.

I'm not at peace until I tell you... this isn't over. The battle ends with your son, not with you. Be careful and be prepared. Your father will try again. Protect the bloodline at whatever cost but know he's coming.... he's coming!" Then she shrieked and disappeared, leaving me visibly shaken as I looked down at my hands.

"Chris...CHRIS!" I'm startled so badly that I faceplant on the floor before I bolt up. "Huh? What?"

"Chris, he's coming. Our son...is coming NOW! Get me to the hospital!" Nessa is doing her labor breathing and there is a big wet spot under her legs.

Her water broke!

"Oh, my goddess!"

The sane thing to do would be to link the hospital staff and have them come get her, but I picked her up, ran down the stairs, and all the way to the infirmary. I link Fitz about our whereabouts and he says he's got me covered with the twins.

I burst through the doors,
"She's…labor…baby…having!" That made no sense,
but they figured it out after she shrieked in pain that the
baby was coming. Several doctors and nurses come to
my aid, one wheeling a chair to place her in to be carted
to labor and delivery. Her cries of anguish are getting
louder as the minutes pass; it'll only be a matter of time
until she's blaming me for doing this to her.

This should be the happiest time of my life, the day my
family starts with this woman, but I am haunted by my
mother's words from the dream.

It isn't over. He'll come for your son.

Not her exact words, but that's what I got from it. I get
that feeling in the pit of my stomach. Fear and
hopelessness. I can't let this happen, I won't. I may have
to find this illusive Papa Ezekiel and kill him myself.

But how do you kill a witch doctor? Miss Ren is my first
line of knowledge, then the other Legacies. I don't know
what my relationship is with my own, but I'm better off.
I sometimes wished that my son wouldn't inherit his
sorcerer, but that's selfish. Unlike his father, he may be
able to control and tame both aspects of himself. But I
also did not sacrifice his power for sinister plans. His
spirit is clean and pure, but I needed to create a plan
knowing what my mother said. This would happen
whether I wanted it or not.

"Alpha Christian, Luna is asking for you." I quickly texted Kayd to let Kam know that Nessa was in labor. It was sad knowing I had no family to relay the good news to. Kam and Kayd grew to be my family, along with the Remington's who saved my life.

"UGHHHH...AHHHH, Chris! Bring your ass here, you did this to me!!!!!! Ahhhh…"

See, right on cue.

Eight hours later:

"Where is he? Where is auntie's baby?"

I pan over to the bassinet and him wrapped up in his baby blue blanket and white knit hat.

"Auntie Kam and Uncle Kayd, meet your nephew and godson, Xander Christian Grey. Seven pounds, nine ounces and born in nine hours."

"Nine hours?! Nessa, you lucky duck, Kay and Kam took 26 hours; consider this a blessing from the Moon Goddess herself." I turn to her to see no amusement on her face.

"Screw this! Next time, IF there is a next time, they can cut me open. This is for the birds!" I lean in so we're both on the screen and I kiss her damp forehead and she looks at me like I'm crazy. "You never looked more beautiful than right now. Thank you, darlin', for our son."

"Aww, that is so sweet!" Kam screams from the screen and giggles.

"Shut up, Kam! But she's right, that is the sweetest thing you could say with me looking like this. I can't wait to see what the future holds for us and our little guy." She kisses me sweetly, but that doesn't tame the churning ocean in the pit of my stomach.

How do I tell her what came in a dream?

That our son, only hours old, already has a long fight ahead of him.

He won't do it alone and he won't be surprised like I was.

I had a dark fate and I'll be damned if he does, too. No chance in hell.

I will FIGHT to the DEATH for my family.

TO BE CONTINUED...

Look out for the 5th and final title of the series

BLOOD BOUND

Stay in Touch!

Email: **authormskeiya@yahoo.com**

FB Author Page: **www.facebook.com/authormskeiya**

Instagram:
www.intstagram.com/author_mskeiya

Bookbub:
www.bookbub.com/profile/s-courtney

Website:
https://www.SCourtneybooks.com

Please look out for the rest of the Bound Series and much more!

THE BOUND SERIES:
Bound to You (#1)
Bound by Destiny (#2)
Blood Bound (#5)
CHARACTER BACKSTORIES:
Unapologetically Nessa (#3)
A Christian Tale (#4)

 # indicates release order

OTHER TITLES:
The Black Aces MC
The Sandman
Assassinated by Love (Book #1 of A Lies & Secrets Production)